Fields of Death

Conrad Jestmore

***

Copyright © 2012 by Conrad Jestmore

All rights reserved

This is a work of fiction. As such, all characters in it do not exist in real life. Names, characters and incidents are products of the author's imagination.

ISBN:978-1479147717

To Mom and Dad. You made me what I am. Thanks.

ALSO BY CONRAD JESTMORE:

River of Murder
(Book 1 in the Jimmy O'Reilly Murder
Mystery Series)

Gooney Birds (Memoir)

Kodak Black and White (Memoir)

A Roadmap to Hope (Poetry)

A Christmas Carol: A Spirited New Musical
(Play)

Available at www.conradjestmore.com

Fields of Death

1

Twenty-seven dead. That was the body count, if you want to look at it statistically. Actually, there were twenty-six dead when I found them, but the twenty-seventh died later.

How he was still alive, I'll never know, and what manner of human being could do such an atrocity to others is beyond my understanding.

I found them on my way back from a skip trace job up to Hutchinson. The September sky was powder white. Not fresh baby powder. It was like kiln residue, dirty, a ceramic piece gone wrong and baked until it crumbled into pale dusty dregs.

The AC had died on my truck and I traveled the back roads, hoping to catch cool breezes off the fields and river lowlands instead of the highway heat and exhaust I'd get if I took 96. It didn't help.

This had been the hottest September in Kansas on record since the 1930s. The month usually starts blazing hot, moderates by the middle, and by the fourth week, you can usually smell fall in the air. It was late September and winter wheat was always in the ground by now, seeded into moist standing stubble.

Instead, I passed disked fields, chunks of baked dry clods, cooked by the sun. Not the deep brown loam of the

Arkansas River basin you would expect, but inert, chalky dirt, almost as pale as the powder-white sky, too dry to accept seed. There weren't even any cattle egrets stalking the fields for insects.

The only thing alive was the field corn that had been irrigated and would be used for fodder, and that was fast disappearing as combines rolled and the harvest got underway.

Both windows were down and I'd been breathing through my mouth because my nostrils felt seared from taking in hot wind, but then my lips crusted and my throat closed off it was so dry. The previous night I had watched the sun go down in a similarly cloudless sky. Instead of the typical glorious sunset of parti-colored streaks, it looked like a hot white flame being extinguished in a vacuum under glass.

My empty water bottle sat in the center caddy. I tried to swallow and couldn't. My soaked tee shirt stuck to my chest, and the road wind coming through the cab didn't dry me out, it only helped crystallize the salt in my sweat. I was only several miles from Chisholm and my bungalow on the west side of town and central air conditioning. But I never made it. At least not as soon as I wanted to. The dead prevented me.

I first got suspicious as I came up on Wiley's farm. Wiley is an old friend of mine who lets me come out unannounced and catfish on his stocked pond. What caught my attention was a semi trailer parked on the dirt road bordering the west side of Wiley's place. There was no tractor attached, which was odd in itself, but there was also no reason for a semi to be parked there in the first place. I slowed down and turned off on to the hard-packed county road, parked behind the trailer, and then got out and walked around it. It had Oklahoma plates and no commercial logo on the side or USDOT number, and the cargo door was padlocked. The left rear tail light was broken.

I don't pack a cell phone, and I figured I'd call Wiley about it when I got home, so I turned and headed back toward my truck, but stopped short. I heard a thump inside the trailer. When I put my ear up close to the door, I thought I heard what sounded like a human voice.

"Is somebody in there?" I pounded on the door. "Hey, anybody in there?" If there was, they couldn't be long for this world.

Then I heard a raspy sounding voice saying something, but I couldn't make out what. It came through the hole where the tail light was broken out. Then I heard it more clearly. *"Ayudame. Ayudame."* Somebody was in there and pleading for help, in Spanish. I ran back to my truck, got the bolt cutters out from my tool box and stood in the blazing sun, working until I finally cut through the padlock. It had to be like a furnace inside the trailer, so it was hard to believe anyone could be alive in there, especially if they'd been locked in for any length of time.

I pulled the latch back and opened one side of the double doors. A rush of heat rolled out, so intense it knocked me backwards, like a back draft from a fire, and with it came an overpowering stench. I gagged, pulled up my tee shirt to cover my nose, and then opened the other door. A partially clothed man lay next to the broken-out tail light, trying to suck air in through the small opening. It looked like he'd kicked it out in an attempt to draw breath. But the worst was yet to come. Over him, I could see a tangled mass of bodies in the dark chamber, with limbs crisscrossing each other. I had no way to even guess how many.

I took the man who was asking for help, slid his body over the trailer's edge and dragged him into the shade side of the trailer. As he lay there in the dust, he began mumbling, *"Los niños. Los niños y las mujeres."*

"Hang on, partner." I looked back into the trailer. It would take a long time to pull all the bodies out. I couldn't even tell if any were alive. I turned back to the man I'd dragged out. "I'm going after help and some water. You hang in there."

"Los niños y las mujeres," he said again, but he seemed to be even more delirious than before.

I had no way of knowing if he'd understood what I just told him, but I jumped in my truck and took off, fishtailing on the hard-pack as I turned around and went back to the highway. Wiley's house was in the opposite direction on the other side of the section, so I took the two-lane blacktop back a quarter of a mile to the Peterson's place. Their station wagon wasn't next to the pole barn and it didn't look like anyone was home, but I knew the house would be unlocked. I knocked loudly, then let myself in to an empty house.

I dialed 911, identified myself, and explained as quickly and as rationally as I could what I'd found and where the trailer and the bodies were located.

"Mr. O'Reilly, we are sending help, but I need you to stay where you are so we can verify-"

I cut the operator off. "I can't do that, Sir. I'm heading back with water now." I hung up, went in the kitchen and dug some empty two liter pop bottles out of the trash, rinsed them out and filled them with tap water.

By the time I got back to the dirt county road, I could hear the first sirens coming the opposite direction from Chisholm. I kneeled down with a bottle of water next to the man I'd dragged out, but I already knew I was too late. I stood next to his body as the Chisholm EMS unit pulled up. Over the next half hour, a series of emergency vehicles arrived from various points, near and far.

*****

Three hours later, it looked like a triage scene from some battle in an unknown war. Medical personnel wore protective masks over their faces and ankle-length blue plastic gowns covered their torsos. Blue vinyl gloves protected their hands. Low cots lined the side of the road, each with a corpse zipped into a body bag, and a temporary morgue had been set up in a refrigerated tractor-trailer unit. It took emergency responders and law enforcement from all three adjoining counties to sort out and begin to deal with the enormity of so much death. Not just the logistics, but the mere acceptance that it had even happened, here, amongst us.

My gaze drifted up, over the line of cocooned bodies and looked out across Wiley's fields. The tall native grasses stood silent in the breezeless heat. Plumes of burnt orange Indian Grass and silvery-blue Big Bluestem with purple turkey foot spikes, displayed a peacefulness that belied the mayhem laying before it. I stepped back, letting the bodies line the edge of my vision and saw the picture for what it was. Fields of death.

Yellow crime scene tape crisscrossed everywhere, and the gawkers and the media had been kept at bay back at the highway, about an eighth of a mile away. But it didn't take too long for both the camera crews and meddling public to work their way around the section through the back roads, and a second front had to be set up to keep them back and away. The story hit the wire services and CNN was the first of the national media to arrive and set up camp.

Initially, I helped pull bodies out of the trailer as emergency vehicles arrived, one after the other. All of the dead were young males. Working age, with what had been strong, able bodies With each victim there was always the prospect of hope, but not one of those twenty-seven was alive. They had been stacked like cordwood, many only partially clothed, in their underwear. They lay amid their discarded clothing that looked like it had been torn off for relief in the killer heat. Crushed plastic water bottles were strewn across the floor, along with unzipped backpacks, their contents spilling out like dangling entrails.

As the last body was being lowered out the trailer doors, I stood alone in the dim light of the death chamber. There were small pinpricks in the sides of the trailer where those who had been slowly suffocating apparently tried to punch holes to breathe through. I found various small objects they must have taken from their backpacks and hacked away at the metal siding in a desperate and vain hope of any brief breath of fresh air.

The little points of sunlight coming through the holes made the dark trailer walls look like night sky, as if stars dotted the interior landscape of this tomb. It was an eerie feeling, at once so seemingly peaceful, as if you wanted to sing to the firmament, and at the same time, it was as if the heavens themselves had opened up to accept these unknown dead, whoever they were, and the false stars were saying goodbye to their earthly existence.

"Jimmy, come down outta there and answer me a few questions."

Alex's voice jolted me out of my thoughts, and I saw his huge frame backlit by bright sunlight at the trailer opening. I climbed down through the open double doors and off the trailer bed. Sheriff Jake Alexander heads up our local three person police force in Chisholm. He's a large man with a booming voice, and both his presence and his voice command respect.

"Alex," I said. "I knew you were around here somewhere, but I hadn't seen you in all the commotion."

"Tell me what happened here, Jimmy. I heard tell you was first on the scene. Was it you that found these poor, unfortunate souls?"

"It was," I said, and I recounted for him, the best I could, how I'd stumbled on the carnage and how I'd gone to phone it in and came back with water in hopes that some might be alive.

"A futile hope, Jimmy. These folks never had a prayer."

"There was one who was alive that I pulled out before I left," I said. "I thought maybe he might make it."

"Who could of done something like this to a fellow human being?" His question begged no response, and after a few seconds of silence, he said, "Tell me. What do you think happened here?"

"It's hard to say. They're all Hispanic, all male, probably undocumented workers. Maybe a human smuggling ring operation gone bad," I said.

"That's the way I read it too, but if it is, if they are illegals, there's gonna be some in these parts that say they deserved it."

"Nobody deserves this kind of fate."

"You know that and I know that," he said. "But you know how some people are around here. There's those that wish the worst on people they're afraid of or don't understand. There's gonna be hell to pay on how this one plays itself out. Thing I can't figure out is how this would happen around here. Most of those rings ship 'em straight out to western Kansas where the feed lots and packing plants are."

"I don't know either, Alex. I just don't know." My response was more about the abject hopelessness of the situation itself than it was about the dilemma he posed.

"I'm deputizing you Jimmy, so's you can help us here, legally. If you'd accepted my offer awhile back to join the force, you'd not only be a deputy, you'd be pulling in an income for it. Think about that."

He'd offered me a job on the force when Phil, a previous deputy, went bad and was taken down from the drug dealings he'd gotten involved in.

"Sorry, Alex, but you know how it is. Like I explained. I just can't." Alex had sympathized, but never fully understood my reaction to my wife's violent death and my withdrawal from the life of crime fighting.

"Okay, but you come by tomorrow. We need to talk some more."

"About me working for you?"

"No. About what went on out here today."

Then he handed me over to KBI agents for more questions and answers. By the time dusk set in, they'd put up portable generators to power floodlights on tripods so the work of dealing with the dead could continue into the night.

2

I didn't go see Alex the next day. It's not that the tragedy and the deaths didn't weigh heavily on my mind or that I thought they didn't need discussing, but I had several skip trace jobs I'd promised Bomber Jackson I would clear his plate of, and I needed to get moving on them.

Bomber Jackson used to work in the aircraft industry, not fly bombers. He's a bail bondsman down on South Seneca in Wichita, and he gives me most of my jobs. So, after I got the AC in my truck fixed and took care of business for Bomber, it was two days later before I was even spending much time at my place in Chisholm, and then an event happened that catapulted the whole tragedy back to the forefront of everyone's mind, not just mine.

By sheer coincidence, not by any planning or manipulation, Lon Claymore had scheduled a campaign rally in Chisholm at the high school for that evening. Lon had grown up in Chisholm, attended its schools and graduated from the high school three years ahead of me, so we'd known each other, at least in a casual way. Years ago, he'd gone on to parlay his family's money into a rather substantial fortune in the oil business and was now a State senator. But he had bigger ambitions, and after switching party affiliation to take advantage of a lack of interest in challenging an incumbent, he won the August primary and was mounting a serious and well-funded campaign for the Fourth District United States Congressional seat.

I'd never liked Lon Claymore, not when he lived here in his younger years, nor now that he lived in his gated estate on the east side of Wichita with his second, and significantly younger wife. But that didn't keep me from attending the rally. I was easily amused by sideshows like these and I didn't plan to miss this one.

The high school gym is not air conditioned and with the bleachers packed and the floor full of occupied folding chairs, the locals were sweltering by the time Lon and his entourage blew in with a grand entrance. A point man came in ahead of them, dressed in a black suit and wearing wrap-around sunglasses. I noticed him because, even though he was involved in what was going on, he acted cool. Not hip-cool, but detached, like he was more of an observer of the action rather than a participant, like a narrator of a Hemingway story.

He signaled, and the high school band struck up a rousing rendition of "Happy Days Are Here Again," and a minute later, the State senator swept through the doors to the gym, smiling and waving, his right hand high in the air as he strode the full length of the court, his PR men or body guards, or whatever they were, trailing him in their immaculate look-alike black suits.

Three local television stations followed the procession, cameras circling off to each side, getting various angles, and the crowd stomped and clapped to the musical beat. Lon Claymore mounted the risers where the band played, and he stepped up to the microphone, now with both arms raised high and hands waving. He's a tall man, and although he's not fat, he's got a big frame and a big gut and a misshapen oval of a face, almost like it had been squeezed in a vice. His eyebrows were perpetually raised, arched as if in constant concern over something. He looked like an over-grown teddy bear or an elongated Pillsbury Dough Boy.

"Thank you. Thank you." The sound system squeaked and reverberated, and he jumped back from it feigning fright and acting like he was going to run away. The crowd screamed, and yelled, "Don't go, Lon. Stay." He re-approached the microphone, signaled for calm, tested the equipment and then said, "Don't worry, I've got it all under control now."

The crowd loved him, not just because he was a local boy made good, but they ate up the entire persona. What I saw as a mere façade, they bought into, part and parcel. He was dressed in tennis shoes, khaki pants and a blue denim shirt with the sleeves rolled up and an open collar. Although he undoubtedly had just gotten out of an air conditioned limousine, he managed to have just enough sweat on his face to look like he was an ordinary workingman, no different than any of them.

"Have you bought your airline ticket for Washington yet?" Someone shouted from high up in the bleachers.

Lon pointed at the person and yelled back, "I'm booking my flight next week. Thank you." The crowd went crazy, applauding and yelling. "You know," he continued, "When I'm sitting in my office on Capitol Hill, each and every one of you, if you should happen to visit Washington, is welcome to come in and sit down and talk with me about any concern you have. And I genuinely mean that."

I think they actually believed him. I never could understand what people see in the guy to like. His pudgy face has an overbite that he's managed to compensate well for, but in doing so, there is a tenseness in his jaw that belies the easygoing manner everyone else sees. It makes me think everything that comes out of his mouth is a lie he's trying to cover up.

"Let's get down to business," he said. "There are some serious concerns we need to talk about. The terrible tragedy that happened earlier this week, right here in Chisholm, represents exactly the things I have been fighting for up in Topeka. These poor people suffered cruel deaths because of the policies of the current administration. I have fought for legislation to deny drivers licenses to illegal aliens. I have fought to change the law so illegals cannot get state tuition rates to our universities. These policies only encourage the influx of illegals, people who take jobs away from you and your sons and daughters, and look at the tragic results of that right here in your community."

Apparently, not everyone present fully agreed with him. Someone yelled out from the middle of the crowd on the floor.

"You haven't accomplished very much. None of that's changed."

The crowd turned and stared in the direction of the offender, and a murmur rumbled through the gym. But Lon was quick, and he shot a response back immediately.

"That's why I want to take your concerns to the national arena. These problems are begging for broader, national responses."

Then, from across the gym in the bleachers, someone yelled, "Who they taking jobs from, Senator? You wouldn't do the work they take on. Neither would I or anybody else here."

This time the crowd started booing, and from where I was standing, leaning against the wall at the back of the gym, I could see two men in suits hustle the antagonizer down the aisle and out the door as Claymore raised his hand and said, "Now folks, there's room for differing views and everybody has a right to be heard."

"Then why was that guy just taken out?" someone shouted.

Claymore looked a little flustered, but that mask came back over his face immediately and a tone of reassurance infused his voice. "I'm going to look into that, Sir. I promise you, it will get my attention."

He pounded on about what he called concerns, and the audience glowed in what they seemed to think was a special attention he was showering on them and them only. But I stood there thinking back to a time when I was in the fourth grade, to an incident that probably colored my view of the person he was from that day forward. An incident he most likely has no recollection of today.

That summer, just after school had let out and I had finished my fourth grade year, I rode my bike up to the Chisholm library and parked it right outside the door. I was on my way to finding some good adventure stories to check out for summer reading. I had Jack London in mind.

That's when Lon and two other older and bigger boys surrounded me.

"Jimmy," one of the others said. "You need to do something for us."

"Yeah," said Lon. "We're coming in to the library with you and we want to hear you walk up to the librarian and say 'Eat shit.'"

"If you don't," said the third one, "we're taking your bike. I'm going to stand here next to it until I get a signal from Lon that you said it."

Then two of them hustled me through the door into the library. I was terrified. I walked along the low rows of shelves pretending to look at books, but I couldn't even read the titles I was so filled with fear.

Lon came up next to me and whispered, "Do it. Do it now or we take your bike and later we'll beat you up."

I was sweating and I kept walking down the rows of books acting like I was looking at them. What is it about fear that clouds our minds and prevents us from thinking?

15

All I had to do was walk up and tell the librarian that three guys were threatening me, yet that never occurred to me.

Lon and his friends finally got bored waiting for me to do their bidding, and they eventually left. They didn't take my bike and they never came to beat me up. But the fear that paralyzed me that day has always remained somewhere within me as a reminder of what those who cruelly wield their power or strength over anyone who is smaller or weaker than them, can do to an individual.

People like Lon put a stain of dread on others that lasts for a lifetime.

The band struck up "Happy Days" again and I saw Lon smiling and waving as he walked to the edge of the risers and stepped down. I beat a hasty exit ahead of the crowd, but outside, as I stood next to the bronze Titan statue of the high school mascot, gauging how I would negotiate my exit from the packed parking lot, Lon Claymore rushed out of the front doors with his retinue of suits following him, and headed for his waiting limousine. He nearly ran into me as he rounded the Titan statue.

"Excuse me," I said and stepped back.

Without saying anything, he sidestepped and kept moving, and then suddenly stopped, maybe thinking he ought to be more considerate of a potential vote. When he turned, there was a flicker of recognition on his face.

"Jimmy? Jimmy O'Reilly, is that you?" he said.

"It is."

He pumped his arm heavily as he shook my hand. It was then I saw what I couldn't see from far back in the gym. His eyes. The eyes of Lon Claymore. They are green and liquid, and they float, never resting on anything, as if they can't focus on specific objects. While his physical hulk of a body exudes warmth, his eyes have a vacant quality, an amorality, as if whatever decision the brain is making at that particular moment will not be based on any perception of what is right or wrong, but only a self-serving interest. That self-interest is the standard for what is morally right in Lon Claymore's life.

"Jimmy, you old son-of-a-gun, it's been years, hasn't it."

"It has," I said.

His suits stepped back on the grass, crossed their arms in front, and waited silently, staring at us.

"How've you been? Hey, I heard you were the one who found all those bodies in the trailer. I just can't imagine what that was like. The horror of it all."

"I had hopes the one I found alive, the one who was talking when I found him, might make it."

"One of them was still alive when you got there?"

"He was."

"You know, I followed your career when you were a cop down in Wichita. And I felt so badly for you when I read about your wife's murder, what's it been, three years now?"

"Six," I said.

"Six. My God, how time flies. My condolences, Jimmy. A terrible tragedy. Just terrible."

"I've learned to deal with it," I said.

"I'm sure you have."

One of the suits stepped forward, the Hemingway narrator-one wearing sunglasses, tapped him on the shoulder and whispered something in his ear.

"Thank you, Baxter," Lon said to him.

Baxter stepped back and became an observer again, detached and stone-faced.

Then Lon said to me, "Listen Jimmy, gotta scram on outta here. We've got another rally down in Valley Center tonight and I don't want to keep the good citizens waiting."

He climbed in the limo, his group getting in a small car behind, and they all sped off into the night as the good citizens of Chisholm began filing out the doors.

18

3

During the two days between my discovery of the trailer and Lon Claymore swooping down upon the town of Chisholm, I was fortunate enough to miss much of the media circus by virtue of being away most of the time on skip trace jobs. Not only CNN, but FOX News and MSNBC had all encamped in the town with their satellite trucks, and there wasn't a motel room to be had in Chisholm's one and only, or in any of the surrounding towns as well.

When I returned, William, my next door neighbor who is a retired railroad worker, filled me in on some of what I'd missed. As I turned in my driveway, he was out in his front yard in a floppy wide-brimmed sun hat, digging dandelions up with an eighteen inch wide spade.

"Don't you think that's kind of overkill?" I said, pointing to the shovel.

"I like to make sure I get all the root, otherwise they pop right back up."

"I guess that makes sense." I said that as I looked at all the gash marks in his lawn.

"Had a lot a visitors whilst you was gone," he said.

"You did? Who came to see you?"

"Not me. You. You the one had the visitors."

I stopped short on the porch, a little wary. "Who might that be, William?"

"Bunch a them T and V guys. News people. NCC and MBCSN."

William got things turned around often, and so I never corrected him unless something important was at stake.

"They came a knocking at your door, one after the other, camera-fellows and them reporters all dressed up in suits and skirts. Then when you didn't answer, they came a bothering me."

"I'm sorry about that."

"Oh, it was kinda fun. I especially liked that pretty blonde. I seen her on the news before. I let her ask me all kind of questions."

"What did they ask you?" I was even more wary now.

"Mostly stuff about you, like did you talk about what you found in the trailer and what you're like, and oh, yeah, what are, what they called your daily habits like? I didn't tell them anything, though, 'cepting some of my own stories about seeing dead people on the tracks when I was working them."

"Thanks. I appreciate that, William." As I opened my front door, he had a last word of warning for me.

"You be careful, Jimmy. They's gonna be back. They's not the kind to give up easy. Course, that pretty one's welcome in my yard anytime."

*****

Three days after finding the twenty-seven dead, I was taking a mid-morning break from computer searches for some skip trace jobs by reading a volume of Irish poetry, when someone tapped lightly on my front door. I opened, and a woman who looked familiar but whom I couldn't quite place, stood looking at me, intensely, as if she was trying to assess some inner quality about me. I didn't say anything, and after several seconds of silence, she finally spoke.

"My name is Inez Gonzalez. Are you Mr. O'Reilly?"

"Yes, I am. Jimmy. Jimmy O'Reilly."

"I have come because Charlotte Daniels told me where you live." She looked me straight in the eyes as she spoke.

"Charlie sent you here?" Charlotte Daniels, Charlie, is a homicide detective for the Wichita Police and we'd been beat partners years ago. Now she was my on-again, off-again, depending upon how libidinous either of us felt at any given moment. Currently, it was an off-again mode.

"*Si Señor*. I mean, yes. She said that you might be able to help me. Help me find someone."

Charlie wasn't in the habit of sending skip trace jobs my way, so I was a little puzzled.

"Why don't you come in, Mrs. Gonzalez." I'd noticed the gold ring on her finger, and she didn't correct me about using the honorific, Mrs. We walked through the living room and sat down in my reading area next to the kitchen. I set the Irish poetry anthology aside. "Is there something I can do for you? Who is it you want me to find?"

She still looked at me in earnest and there was a sincerity about her that could not be mistaken. She was also a visual display of everything an Anglo might consider stereotypically Hispanic. Middle-aged, she was heavy, rounded, and I could see she was once a striking beauty when she was younger. Her jet-black hair had a few wisps of gray in it, and she wore it pulled back and tied, which only emphasized the fullness of her face and lips even more. She dressed in a plain, cotton print, one-piece dress, its light color contrasting with her olive skin and dark eyes. When she wasn't staring at me while talking, she looked away, as if in deference or out of an expected subservient compliance.

"Yes, there is," she said. "I want you to find who it is killed my brother."

This set me back for a moment, then I said, "Mrs. Gonzalez, Charlie- I mean Detective Daniels may have misled you. I don't do that kind of work anymore. I do what is called skip trace jobs. Missing persons, people who have jumped bail. That sort of thing. In fact, I mostly just work for bail bondsmen."

"You are a licensed private investigator, no?"

"Yes, but as I said, I-" I interrupted myself and changed tactics. "Why don't you tell me about your situation and maybe I can recommend someone."

She was hesitant at first and took her time, and then finally began. "Last week, my brother Julio was found. He was found... dead. Dead in that abandoned trailer just outside of Chisholm."

Suddenly I remembered her. She had arrived a few hours after we found the bodies and I'd seen her escorted from corpse to corpse, the worker unzipping each plastic bag, until she obviously recognized one and knelt down in grief next to it.

"Someone did that to him with intent. I mean intentionally. I'm sorry, my English is not so very good."

"You speak English well." Better than many of us locals I thought. "I'm sorry for your troubles, Mrs. Gonzalez. This must be a very difficult time for you." I could see she was steeling herself to hold back tears.

"I have money, Mr. O'Reilly. I am able to pay you." She started to reach into her purse.

"That's not necessary. Money isn't really the issue here, at least at this point. These deaths are being investigated. Besides the local authorities, KBI and Immigration are also involved. You need to let them handle this."

"But they will not listen to me. They do not believe me, when I tell them-" She looked at me in that appraising way again, and then said, "Detective Daniels said you are a man who can be trusted."

"I believe I can be."

"Then I will tell you all of the story. I could only tell them part of it, and perhaps that is why they would not believe me. Julio and his wife Maria had two children and they are missing. All three of them. I sent two thousand dollars each to them in Mexico, eight thousand dollars in total, for all four of them so they could come to this country."

"Illegally?"

"Yes, illegally." She looked away, but there was no guilt in her face.

"Maybe what you ought to do is start with the Mexican authorities. Maria and the children might still be there, with other relatives."

"No *Señor*. Julio was my younger brother, by ten years. Our parents are both dead and we have no other family there. Besides, Julio would never have left them behind. This I know for certain and I know it *en mí corazón*. In my heart I know this."

Then I remembered the man I'd pulled out of the trailer who was still alive. *"Los niños,"* he had muttered before he died. Over and over, *"Los niños, los niños y las mujeres."* I had thought him delusional from heat and dehydration for rambling on about children and women in an almost mantra-like way.

But then an image came to me of the inside of the trailer. The personal effects of the dead had been scattered about, and although all the bodies had been male, it suddenly dawned on me that some the items were definitely female possessions.

"Look." She pulled a picture from her purse and shoved it in my hand. "This is Little Julio, seven years old.

And Elena, she has twelve years. They are beautiful children, and I fear for them. And this. This is Maria, also beautiful."

I looked at their images. They were beautiful children, and given what I knew and she didn't, about what the dying man had said, I feared for them too.

"Listen. I can't really promise you anything, but I will make some inquiries. I'm not taking the case, mind you, but I will ask a few questions on your behalf." She reached into her purse and asked how much, but I stopped her again. "I hope you won't take this wrong, but I would like to see your Green Card."

"Yes, of course."

I verified her legal status as a Resident Alien, and then asked another potentially embarrassing question. "And Mr. Gonzalez. He is not with you today?" I was suspecting he might be here illegally.

"No. My husband is no longer alive. He died two years ago, in what you call an industrial accident."

"I'm sorry," I said. I thought of all the horror stories I'd heard about working conditions for immigrant labor and how powerless the victims were. "Write down your name and address and how I can contact you. I'll let you know if I find anything out. One way or the other, I'll let you know."

When she handed me the information, I noted she lived at a rural address several miles north of town.

"Thank you Mr. O'Reilly. Detective Daniels was correct." She was looking me in the eyes again. "I know I can trust you."

After she left I picked up the poetry I'd been reading. It was an anthology of Irish poets who had been executed for their part in the 1916 Easter Uprising to overthrow the British occupation. The strange thing was, little of their poetry had anything to do with politics or war. It mostly was about beauty, or much of it was introspective.

The poem I'd left off with was Thomas MacDonagh's "O Star of Death," and the stanza that jumped out at me read:

> Wisdom's voice is the voice
> Of a child who sings to a star
> With a cry of, Hail and rejoice!
> And farewell to the things that are,

A shiver ran down my spine, and I read the rest of the poem before I left to go downtown and talk to Sheriff Alexander.

4

I drove across Sixth Street to Commercial and walked in the low blond brick building that sits a block north of the town square, and serves as our city jail and police station. Alex sat at his desk in the large open area where all three officers worked. Open manila files cluttered his desk, and he studied one intently.

"Alex." I greeted him.

"Jimmy." He said back.

"Sorry I haven't been by sooner. I know you wanted to talk some more about what happened. You making any progress with it?"

"I'm not too involved, other than helping out KBI and Immigration. This is pretty much their baby, and they don't seem to want to keep me too much informed. I do know they've located a couple of relatives of the victims and questioned them. We're in contact with Mexican authorities on body retrieval, but if they got any leads on who done this or how or why, I haven't been told about it."

"Do you still hold with the human smuggling ring theory?" I said.

"Seems likely to me, but I'm still puzzled about why this all came down here."

"Maybe," I said, "they'd started up from Texas, using the I-35 corridor as a route, then had to alter plans because of some unforeseen difficulties and finally decided to get rid of their cargo rather than deal with whatever predicament they were in."

"Could be."

"You heard anything about kids or adult women being involved in this?"

"Kids? What do you mean?"

I told him about the man who died outside the trailer and what he had said before he died. But I didn't tell him about Inez Gonzalez coming to see me and what she said about her niece and nephew. He hadn't heard anything about children or women, so I asked him to let me know if anything turned up. I was saying my goodbyes when he took a call and motioned for me to sit back down. He finished the call, and then turned to me.

"We got us another body," he said.

"Another body?"

"Yep. Number twenty-eight."

"Hispanic?"

"No. This one's Caucasian. That was Jack calling it in. He's on patrol and found it out east of town. Want to ride along?"

"Sure, why not?"

As we headed out the door, he put another dig in. "You know, I could be paying you for this. Take that open spot on the force we haven't filled yet. Job's yours, you know."

I didn't bother responding.

He pulled the cruiser out from the alley and onto Commercial and we drove through town past all the media satellite trucks parked around the square. They hadn't caught up with me yet, but they still hung around draining every possible story they could from Chisholm.

Three miles east of town Alex turned down a dirt road and pulled up behind Jack Sampson's cruiser. Jack stood next to a culvert with his hands on his hips studying the scene.

"What we got here?" said Alex.

"Dale was checking fence along here and discovered this. He was headed back to call it in when I happened by and he flagged me down."

We looked below us, and the shoulders and head of a male body, face down, protruded out of the culvert.

"Looks like somebody tried to stuff him in there but he got stuck and they gave up," said Jack.

We stepped down to the body and could see a single bullet entry wound in the back of the head.

"It looks like a nine. One shot from the rear," I said. I looked up and out over the disked field with its lumps of overturned earth. It looked like it was ready to receive a body, and be turned back over to complete a burial. Another field of death, I thought.

"Well, let's get busy," said Alex. "Looks like we got us some work to do here."

When we freed the body from the culvert and pulled it out, the left hand was covered in blood. We looked closer and the little finger had been cut off.

"I'd say that's pretty curious," said Alex.

Jack stared open mouthed. "Darndest thing I've ever seen. Dead man shot in the back of the head, with one finger cut off clean as a whistle, and him stuffed in a culvert out in the country next to a field."

"Not something I've ever seen before either," I said.

By the time the body was bagged and taken away, there was very little we knew. A white male, no ID; not recognized as anyone from anywhere around here; shot with a 9 mm in the back of the head; little finger of left hand severed; dressed in jeans and a work shirt; pockets, except for one item, emptied of everything. The one item was the curious part. Whoever stripped him of ID and belongings missed one thing. In the small watch pocket of his Levis was a key with no number or manufacturer's name.

I sat silent as we drove back into town. When I told Lon Claymore outside the high school that I had learned to deal with my wife's murder, I was being truthful. I had finally moved on with my life. But the image of her lying face down in a pool of blood in a convenience store cooler, a victim of a botched robbery, will never leave me, and it is undoubtedly the reason I resigned from the WPD and divorced myself from the frontlines of violence. I know Alex can't understand how I prefer simple skip trace jobs to coming to work for him, but that's part and parcel of my way of being my own detached participant.

I had Alex drop me off at the town square when we got back to Chisholm. I needed to pick up a loaf of Italian at the bakery, but before I could cross the street, a cameraman stepped in front of me, lens aimed squarely at me, and a young, clean-shaven man shoved a microphone in my face while speaking rapidly.

Oh, God, I thought, they've finally found me.

"This is Henderson Looper coming to you live from Chisholm, Kansas, with our man on the street interviews, trying to get candid views of local inhabitants as to how their town has been impacted by recent events. What is your name?"

If he didn't know, I wasn't about to tell him, so I affected my best hick accent, a sort of combined imitation of Walter Brennan and Andy Devine.

"Well, Sir," I said, my voice squeaking a little. "You said this here is one a them live interviews?"

"Yes it is. Are you a resident of Chisholm?"

"Yes Sir, I am." My stance was even becoming Walter Brennanish as my elbows jutted out and I stood like I walked with a hitch in my git-along.

"How have these recent tragic events affected you and the residents here in this small mid-west town?"

"Well," I stared off into space and put a deeply pensive look on my face. "I cain't say they rightly have.

Around these here parts, Hendyson, is it alright I call you Hendyson, I see you every day on the tellyvision?" He smiled weakly at me. "Around here, we're pretty darn well used to excitement."

"This seems like such a peaceful, sleepy little village to me," he said.

"Hell, no. Oops, can I say that on TV? Just look around you. We're proud of this place and all that goes on here. Our high school Titans are the state champs. See, there's the great symbol of our Chisholm High Titans."

I pointed up toward the top of the water tower in the town square, which hadn't been painted in years, so the last two letters were faded and what should have appeared as TITAN COUNTRY with a warrior's helmet in the middle, actually read TIT COUNTRY. The water reservoir is oblong with the outflow device on the bottom looking somewhat like a nipple, so here was national news zooming in, live, on an object that looked like a giant boob with an advertising label.

The cameraman panned up on the logo and before he realized what it said, I got in, "Yep. Hunters coming through town during quail season think they found paradise."

The camera quickly came back down and Looper backed away, fumbling and saying, "Ah, yes, well, thank you, Mister... ah, Mister... well thank you..."

But I wasn't about to let him get off so easily. I stepped into camera view and before Looper realized what had happened, I grabbed the microphone from him and turned the tables. I dropped the Walter Brennan accent and took on the mellifluous baritone range of a news anchor.

"Mr. Looper, as an outsider, what are your impressions of our fair city?"

"What? Hey, you can't-"

The cameraman got a strange look on his face, like he didn't know whether to fish or cut bait. He decided to fish and kept the camera rolling.

"I'm certain," I said, maintaining the fake baritone, "all those viewers out there in TV land would like to hear your incisive insights on Middle America. What do you-"

But Looper frantically signaled the cameraman to cut the video, grabbed the mic from me and announced, "Sorry folks, we are experiencing technical difficulties with our video feed. I am returning you to our studios in…"

By then I was entering the bakery and smiling smugly to myself.

*****

When I got home dusk was settling in, but the heat had not abated. The lights were on inside my house, which meant Janie was there doing her chores. Janie Clayton was a ninth grader at the high school and I hired her to come over as needed, a few times a week to water the herbs and perennials on my terrace and clean up around the house. She called out from inside my pantry when I came in.

"Is that you Mr. O?"

"Yes it is, Janie."

"I'm in the pantry taking stock for you."

She came out, her dark hair and oval face peering around the door and preceding her skinny body. You couldn't tell by looking at her how strong she was and what physical power she possessed in her pitching arm when she played softball.

She adopted her motherly tone she always uses when admonishing me.

"You've let your supplies dwindle again, Mr. O." Then she squinted at me like she always does, for emphasis, when talking directly to me. "You still have plenty of that Italian olive oil you import, but your

31

domestic stock is running short, so you'd better put in an order to that California company. And you only have one can of your San Marzano tomatoes left."

"Thanks. You're the best Janie." I squinted back, unconsciously, and then realized what I was doing. I really didn't know what I would do without her.

"I'm sorry I haven't been here for several days, but I made the JV volleyball team and we started practices."

"Congratulations," I said.

"Yeah, I guess. I had hopes of making varsity, but I'm not tall enough. Maybe next year."

"JV is pretty good for a freshman, Janie."

"I know. By-the-by, Mr. O."

Sometimes I thought this skinny kid was a sixty year old woman the way she talked and mothered me.

"Something kind of strange happened a little while ago," she said. "I'd just finished watering the rosemary and basil on the terrace, came back in, and I saw somebody walk across your backyard."

"Who was it?"

"I don't know, but he caught a glimpse of me through the window. He kind of just stood there for a second, like he was casually observing things, you know, like he was standing on the sideline at a football game or something. Then he took off. He was weird looking, wearing a dark suit and those strange sunglasses that come all the way around your head."

"Baxter?" I said, thinking about the man I'd seen with Lon Claymore.

"Who's Baxter? Somebody you know?"

"No, he's not, and Janie, you need to call down to Sheriff Alexander's when something like that happens."

"I know I should have, but he left right away, so I didn't think too much about it until later. Oh, Ty was asking after you."

Ty, Tiresias, is my blind Ornate Box turtle I rescued who lives in my back yard. "Asking after me?" I asked.

"Yeah, you know. He sort of comes out of hiding and makes his presence known. Then he just looks up like he's expecting you to be there. I think he has something to tell you."

"Sure. Like he can actually talk."

"Well, you never know. Say, I gotta go. I still have homework. They sure pile it on in high school."

"Let me drive you home." She lived on the other side of town a block from the town square. "It's getting dark, and what with that man having come around, let's be on the safe side."

On the drive over, she said, "You know that book of Seamus Heaney poems you gave me last summer? I was reading some of those again last night, and he's very confusing with all those Greek names like Cassandra and Clytemnestra and Agamemnon. I think I like those Yeats poems better. They're easier to understand."

"Give him a chance, Janie. He's tough, but he's worth it."

"I did like the one called 'Mint.' It reminded me of your herb garden with all its smells, and the one line in it about letting things that survive go free is really true. I believe in that. Kind of like you did with Ty."

When I let Janie out, her puppy, W.B., was waiting patiently on the porch for her and came bounding out to greet her. As I drove back to my place, the final stanza of "Mint" came back to me. Part of it read, "The smells of mint go heady and defenceless /…Like the disregarded ones we turned against / Because we'd failed them by our disregard."

When I fell asleep later, I was still thinking of those lines, and the man who kept muttering *"los niños"* over and over, and the picture of young Julio and Elena. Ones we'd failed by our disregard.

5

The next morning, despite the heat, I got up early and did a section run, one mile west out of town, one mile north, then one east and one south back into town. As I passed dry and empty fields, thoughts of both the MacDonagh and Heaney poems played over and over in my mind, intermixing: children singing to stars and saying farewell, and our own failures of those in need, simply by omission and disregard. And then Inez Gonzalez' photo of her niece and nephew intruded into the poetic images.

Despite the words and images that pulled at me and haunted my mind, I intended to call Mrs. Gonzalez when I got home and tell her there was nothing I could do for her. My inquiry with Alex, as well as a few calls to my contacts at KBI and other agencies netted no information at all.

I tried to think of the words to tell her as I walked up my drive, sweaty and breathing heavily from my run. That's when I noticed the front door open and I thought it curious that Janie would be here two days in a row.

"Janie?" I called out as I entered the living room. "Janie. What are you doing-"

My inquiry was cut short. Baxter sat in a chair in my reading area, calmly staring off into space.

"What the hell are you doing in here?"

He didn't bother to rise. He just sat there in his dark suit, sans sunglasses. "We have some business to discuss."

"Most people make appointments."

"This is one of those, 'I'm sort of in the neighborhood' things."

"What can I do for you, Baxter? By the way, is that your first or last name?"

He didn't bother answering the second question. "Mr. Claymore would like to see you."

"Tell him to just drop in any ole time. Everybody else does. So, if you'll excuse me, I have-"

"Now. He wants to see you now."

"My time's a little tight at the moment, and as you can see, or smell, I desperately need a shower."

"I said he wants to see you now. Let's go." He finally stood up.

"Baxter, let's you and I play a little game of Suppose," I said. "This is how it works. Suppose, for example, I don't want to go right now?"

He casually opened his suit coat and displayed a shoulder holster with handgun. "Suppose, you change your mind," he said.

"I don't Suppose you'd really use that, here, would you?"

"I don't Suppose you'd care to find out."

It was the shortest game of Suppose I had ever played. The ride to Lon Claymore's estate at least allowed me to cool off in the air-conditioning of Baxter's black Towne Car. He drove with sunglasses on and is not what you would call a conversationalist, so it was a pretty quiet ride. We skirted the city limits of Wichita, passing new subdivisions encroaching on old pastures and wheat land, all baking in the September sun.

When we drove up to the gated entrance on the far east side of Wichita, he clicked some electronic device and the gate swung open. We drove up a winding paved drive, under canopied oaks and maples and past a manicured lawn that looked as if it might have stretched to Texas and back.

We parked in front of a sprawling ranch house, one that looked like it was built in the fifties, but probably was a recent imitation of the style and obviously wrapped back and around itself.

Baxter opened the Towne Car door for me. Oh, he was such a gentleman. "Get out," he said, and we walked through a wide double door entrance and into a gaping entryway of Travertine marbled floors and walls. He motioned me to step down into a sunken room that overlooked a broad expanse of private lake with a boathouse and dock.

As I stood looking out over it, Lon Claymore swept into the room and extended his hand to me, shaking it violently.

"Jimmy, you SOB. Hell-of-a nice gesture, you coming out here on such short notice," he said. His elongated dough face jiggled and his eyes were unfocused.

"I didn't have much choice," I said. My voice was flat. "Baxter here, insisted. Rather forcibly. He has an enforcement clause inside his coat there."

Lon looked at him. "Baxter," he said. "There was no need for that. Jimmy and I are old friends. We go way back."

"Yeah, way back," I said. I wondered whether he remembered a similar incident, way back, of coercion, in the fourth grade at the library. Eat shit, I wanted to say.

"Jimmy, we need to talk." He dismissed Baxter with a wave of his hand, and the black suited, sun-glassed aide disappeared. "You want a drink?" He rang a bell, something I thought only happened in "B" movies, and a servant appeared. "Pedro," he said, "Bring us each a scotch and soda."

"Plain water for me," I said. "It's a little early and besides, I'm replenishing electrolytes from my workout." I raised an arm and displayed a sweat ring on my shirt.

His servant vanished and I asked Lon, with some sarcasm, if Pedro had a Green Card. He ignored me.

"I am concerned with what you witnessed at the unfortunate debacle of the Hispanics that were found dead."

"And?..." I said.

"Well, let's cut to the chase, Jimmy. You've been asking around. Questions, you know."

Pedro returned with a tray of two drinks. Lon picked up the scotch and soda. I drained the plain water in one gulp.

"Thank you, Pedro," I said. "By the way, do you have a Green Card, Pedro?"

His eyes widened and he looked at Lon, turned and left quickly.

"Jimmy, you need to leave the resolution of these details to the authorities. They know what they're doing and they will get to the bottom of it all."

"Like how twenty-seven people were butchered?" I said.

"That... and, well, you need to quit asking questions about children. The children will be taken care of by the authorities."

"What do you know about children?"

"Lay off it, Jimmy. Just lay off it."

"You know," I said. "You sit here in this maze of a rat's den overlooking your personal lake, and you have no idea of how the average worker gets by. How do you pay for this place, Lon? You can't finance it on a State senator's salary. Where do you get it?"

"My business, I... I-"

"My business, my ass. You-"

"Why Lonnie, you didn't tell me we had company."

Lon's wife stood on the step above the sunken room, in a slouched stance and holding a rocks glass, empty except for the ice. She was a slim brunette, attractive except

38

for the eyes that were glazed over from the early morning booze. She was also considerably younger than Lon. She held out her glass.

"Lonnie, be a good boy and pour me another bourbon."

He took the glass and set it down. "Go back to the solarium. I'll be there in a few minutes," he said.

"Aren't you going to introduce me to this handsome gentleman?" She held out her hand, limp and hanging down. "My name is Charlene. And you-"

Lon grabbed her arm, twisting it and pulling her up the step and out of sight. Then I heard, "Pedro, see that Mrs. Claymore gets settled in the solarium."

When he returned, he said, "You'll have to excuse my wife, she-"

"Lon." I set my empty water glass down. "I didn't like you as a kid, and I don't like you now. Call someone to take me home. Preferably not Baxter. We don't have a lot in common." I walked up the step and to the front door, then turned back to him.

"Solarium?" I said.

6

"Hell's Bells, Jimmy. I think I got something for you on that kid thing you was askin' about. Give me a call. My cell number."

It was Alex's voice mail I had returned to when I got home, and all the way back I had been thinking about Lon Claymore's statement, that the authorities would take care of the children. What children was he talking about? And what did he know about any children and how did he know it? Now, all of a sudden, I had two possible leads for Inez Gonzalez.

I dialed Alex's number.

"Hey Jimmy. I'm out here to the Jimmerson place. They got two Hispanic little ones sitting in their living room and we don't know who they are. They don't speak English so we can't find anything out about them."

"Male or female? How old?" I asked.

"One of each, and Hell, I don't know. A kid's a kid. The girl's a little older though."

"I'll be right out." The genders and possible age difference fit Inez Gonzalez' niece and nephew.

"You can't talk Spanish, Jimmy."

"I speak a little. Maybe I can find out something." I hung up before he could say anything and was out the door, wondering if, and hoping all the way there, that it might be Elena and Little Julio.

When I left my drive, a black car I didn't recognize started up across the street and followed me, staying well back, as if that could fool me. It turned north on the county road when I turned and headed toward the Jimmersons. It wasn't a Towne Car, so it probably wasn't Baxter.

John and Sally Jimmersons' place was just a section north of where I had found the trailer. It's an old two story farm house with several out-buildings. When I got there, Alex's cruiser sat cross-wise in the gravel turn-around by the barn, and as I turned in, the follower kept on going, out of sight down the road. My over-active imagination must have got the better of me.

They called to me to come on in, and there in the dining room sat two of the cutest kids I'd seen in a longtime. They were not Elena and Little Julio, however. I had no good news for Inez Gonzalez.

They sat wolfing down ham sandwiches that Sally Jimmerson had made for them, and a pitcher of milk stood nearly empty, on the table next to them. The girl's feet barely touched the floor, and the boy's legs dangled loosely from his chair seat. They ignored me as they kept eating.

Alex's hulking frame sat stooped and scrunched up on a short stool as he tried to come down to their level, and the Jimmersons sat opposite the kids, in silence.

"Aren't they just as cute as a button?" said Sally.

"Yes they are," I said. "At least, if a button can be cute, then they certainly are." Everyone just stared at me. "Cute, that is." More silence.

I cleared my throat and tried a new approach. "John," I said." What's the story here?" John was dressed in his overalls, obviously ready for a day's work on the farm.

"Well, I'd been cleaning chicken coops all morning and when I went to go back to the barn, I heard this rustling sound up in the loft. I mean, loud rustling, not like barn mice would make. When I go up to take look, there's these two young 'uns. They was huddling in the corner, real scared-like, so's I got Sally here, and she brought 'em out some of her chocolate chip cookies, and eventually we coaxed 'em on into the house. They haven't said word one. Eating us out of house and home though."

"I tried talking to them," said Alex. "I said something like, 'Bonus dee-az,' but they just stared at me. The girl giggled, though. That's the only sound we've heard out of them."

"Bonus dee-az? I doubt they understood much of that, Alex. Let me have try," I said. I sat down next to them and smiled. They smiled back. "See Alex. That's how it's done. We're already communicating."

I shifted in the chair a little, smiled bigger, pointed to myself and then, in my stilted, basic Spanish, said, "*Me llamo Señor* O'Reilly. My name is Mr. O'Reilly," I translated for the benefit of the others. No response. "*¿Como se llama?* What's your name?" Still no response.

Alex laughed. "Don't look like they're understanding much a what you're saying either."

"No, it's kind of like your dog, Alex. He understands alright, he just chooses not to respond." I tried a few more attempts in my basic Spanish, all with no reaction.

"I have an idea," I said. "I'd like to bring over a woman that speaks their native language and is of their heritage. Maybe they would trust her and open up."

"They're cute as a button, but they can't stay here," said Sally, and John nodded in agreement.

"Take them down to the station, Alex."

"I can't keep them there. Besides, I doubt they're legals. I got to turn 'em over to Immigration."

"Whoa, Alex. Don't jump the gun here. You know as well as I do, that would be a pretty grim fate for them.

We have a chance to find out if there is a connection to all the deaths here. Don't pass that up."

"Well, how soon could you get this woman?"

I used the Jimmersons' phone and called Inez Gonzalez, telling her what had happened. I also called Laura Bascome and asked her if she could come. When I walked back in the dining room, everyone still stared in silence.

"I'll meet you at the station in an hour, along with the woman. Her name is Inez Gonzalez. I also asked Laura Bascome to come. She's a CASA volunteer and may have some insights for us."

"One hour?" said Alex as I walked out the door.

"At the station," I said.

I never made it to the station.

7

When I came to, I sat tied to a metal chair on a dirt floor that radiated heat. My head throbbed and my throat was as dry as an empty coffee cup. I tried to focus, but every joint in my body ached. I had no idea how I'd gotten there and no recollection of what happened.

It took a while, but eventually, I could tell I was in a shed. A metal shed with no window, no open door and no ventilation. The only light came from what was probably a twenty-five watt bare light bulb in the corner. The interior of the shed was blazing hot.

The only door opened and a lone male entered and stood before me, arms crossed. He had on jeans and a flannel shirt and wasn't even sweating.

"O'Reilly," he said. "We need to talk."

"Everybody wants to talk." My voice was raspy. "What's the price of a drink around here? Cheap, I hope. Just like talk."

"You want something to drink? What would you like?"

"A Margarita, maybe. No salt." He didn't laugh.

"You play your cards right, we'll get you some water. You have to agree to a few things first."

"Such as?"

"Such as, it's time to get back to your skip trace work and leave all this other business alone."

"What other business?"

"That's not a good answer." He pulled out a switchblade and flicked it open, weighing it in his hand.

"Okay," I said. "Tell Baxter that enough is enough. Cut the funny business."

"Who's Baxter?"

"Yeah. Sure. Do you report directly to Claymore or is Baxter your boss?"

"Don't know any Baxter and I don't know any Claymore. You ready to get down to brass tacks now?"

"Who are you?"

He scraped his thumb across the knife blade, checking it's sharpness. "Let's just say I represent several individuals who have employed me to see that their interests are protected."

"And what might their interests be?"

"I don't think you get this, O'Reilly. A lot of industry around here depends on employment. Employment that requires certain kinds of individuals at certain wage levels. Your actions are interfering with that."

"Illegals?"

He walked around to the back of the chair, holding the knife even with my neck as he moved. I could feel the blade behind me, hovering next to my occipital bone where it meets my spine. Then, suddenly, his arm dropped and I felt the tension as the knife blade sliced through the rope binding my arms. My arms dropped free to my sides.

"Stand up." He walked back around to my side, picking up a two-by-four as he went. "Get back to your day job. Period."

Then he reared back and swung the two-by-four, a crushing blow to my solar plexus. I dropped to my knees, gasping for breath.

"That's just to show you we mean business."

*****

The next time I came to, I was laying in the alley behind Chisholm's police station. When I hobbled in through the back door, Alex looked up from his desk at me and shook his head.

"You're a little late, Jimmy."

"Sorry. I got unexpectedly detained." I propped myself up by leaning on his desk.

"You look like shit. Somebody beat you with a stick?"

"As a matter of fact..." I trailed off and sat down. "How late am I? For the meeting, I mean."

"That was three hours ago. That Gonzalez woman is great. Got them kids to open right up and boy did we learn a lot. And Laura, she knows the ins and outs of CASA and all these other support services I never knew nothing about, and how to get right to it and who to go to for protection."

"What did you find out?"

"Them kids was on that trailer, along with a bunch more. Probably twelve to fifteen or so. Gonzalez' two relations was among 'em. The kids knew them by name. Thing is, all the children were off-loaded somewheres, a few days ago. The kids didn't know where and they didn't know when. They kept them in a locked room, and these two had escaped. Been scared, hungry and on the run."

"Can I see them?"

"That's the bad news. They're gone."

"To CASA already?"

"No. I mean gone. Vanished. The three of us went into the private office to make the phone calls, and when we come back out, they was nowhere to be found. Esteban and Esperanza, that's their names. Jack, me, all of us have been out trying to find any trace of them we could. It's like they never even existed. Esteban and Esperanza."

I stood. "I've got to get out and help-"

"You got to get home and get some rest." He sat me back down. "I found your truck on the way back, a mile down the road from the Jimmerson place, keys still in it. I knew something was wrong then. And when you didn't show up... well, Jack brought your truck back and parked it at your house. That's where I'm taking you now. Fill me in on what happened on the way."

8

I slept through the night and when I awoke the next morning, my joints and muscles still throbbed with pain. I rolled over, gingerly, and looked at the alarm clock. It was noon. I heard someone moving in my living room and an old Linda Ronstadt CD was playing. When I peeked through a slat in my window blinds, I saw Laura Bascome's red Vette in my driveway, hardtop removed.

Laura and I had been good friends in college, both of us getting degrees in Criminal Justice. She now taught Administration of Justice courses at Wichita State University, and while we were not partners in the crime fighting business, her Aikido and marksmanship skills had saved my butt more than once. She is also a bone expert with a PhD. in anthropology. What you would call a well-rounded girl.

I hobbled into my living room and she looked up from her cup of coffee at me. She was dressed in a teal silk outfit with a mauve and black accent scarf, all complimented by her long flowing auburn hair. Oh yeah, I forgot to mention her sense of fashion.

She just stared at me and shook her head. Somehow, I always feel guilty in her presence, like a little boy who'd done something he wasn't supposed to. And Laura was really good about needling me and never letting me forget my shortcomings. Linda Ronstadt sang "You're No Good" on the CD that played.

"Nice choice in music," I said.

"It reminded me of you. So, who beat you up this time O'Reilly, and what did you do to tick them off?"

"Give me a break, Laura. It wasn't my fault. Let me get some coffee and I tell you all about it."

"Not till you give up some poetry. You know me. I don't work for free. You have to recite something special for my favors."

"As always." I limped over to my reading area and picked up the MacDonagh poem, "O Star of Death," and read the stanza about a child singing to a star and saying farewell to all that was known.

Laura shook her head again, but this time not as an admonition to me. "Oh my, O'Reilly. What is the world coming to. Talk about loss of childhood innocence."

"So, I take it there has been no word on the two kids."

"No. Nothing."

She sat there on my couch, dejected and forlorn. If there was one thing that could get Laura down, it was social injustice and the wrongs committed against the helpless. But she usually didn't stay down long. She always came up fighting, taking the side of those who had no voice for themselves.

"You'd better sit down," she said. "I need to fill you in."

I got some coffee, sat across from her and listened to details of a world I really didn't want to know anything about or acknowledge even existed.

"Do you have any idea," she began, "of the extent of human trafficking?"

"I know it's out there. The shirt I'm wearing probably was made by a sweathouse slave in the Fareast somewhere. And the chocolate I ate for desert last week probably was touched by a child slave somewhere in the world."

"This isn't only sweathouse slavery. I'm talking about prostitution and pornography. People being stolen and sold for sex. We are talking millions of people worldwide, but it is big business right in our own backyard, too."

"Seems like women always get the short end, don't they."

"We're not just talking females. Forty-eight percent of human trafficking consists of male victims. And get this. Twenty-eight percent are six to eleven year olds. Thirteen percent are under six years of age."

"Oh, come on Laura. What would they want with little kids. What would anybody-"

"You really are naive, for someone who's spent so many years in law enforcement. Child porn pictures, porn movies and sex. That's why they want them. And that's why we have to find these kids fast, before they are dealt off to someone who will use them. If they haven't already, that is."

Now I was dejected. I sat grim-faced. "What do we do? I mean, where do we go from here?"

"You're the PI. And you're always asking me what to do? Honestly O'Reilly, I wonder about you sometimes."

"Yeah, well you always seem to have the answers." I mocked her, but she didn't get it.

"Wichita. I think we go to Wichita," she said.

"What you mean *we* Kimosabe?"

"You think you're the Lone Ranger and Tonto all rolled into one, don' you? Give me a break, O'Reilly. Here's what I think. Take it or leave it. These people operate wherever and whenever they can, hidden from view. Yes, they operate in rural areas. But given the circumstances, they are going to have the best cover in the

50

city. If these kids haven't already been dealt off to someone yet, they are probably being held somewhere in Wichita."

"Okay, but the locals as well as the Feds are already looking. You think we can do better than them? Besides, we don't have any leads or anywhere to look."

"You got contacts. Charlie. Give your girlfriend a call."

"Charlie is not my girlfriend. She's just... well." I trailed off. The word girlfriend irked me and made it sound like I was in middle school. "Why do you always make me feel like I'm a little boy, Laura?"

"Maybe because you are. At heart, you've never grown up, O'Reilly. You're a middle-aged man who's never grown up. Sometimes I think you are still in kindergarten. It wouldn't surprise me if you had cookies and milk, and then rolled out a rug and took a nap on the floor right now."

I stood up and walked out through my French doors onto my terrace and herb garden, just to get some air. Tiresias wandered out of the basil plants and onto the flagstone terrace and stretched his neck out of his turtle shell, looking up at me. His wizened face and wise, sightless eyes penetrated deep into me. Janie was right. He did have something to tell me. I wished I could understand him.

Then, something happened that just sort of snapped within me, and the next thing I knew, Laura stood in the open French doors staring at me and said, "What truck ran over you?"

"Can you get an epiphany from a turtle?" I said. "Because I think I just did." I looked down at Tiresias, but he was gone. Damn, turtles are fast when they want to be. "Ty just told me something."

"Okay, Dr. Doolittle. Walk with the animals. Talk with the animals. What's the word from the wild?"

"Make fun of me if you want," I said. "But I know where we need to go."

9

We pulled up in my truck behind a twenty-eight foot long, silver Airstream luxury trailer. It had taken me about an hour of wandering alleys and searching the usual spots to find it, and I had endured a full hour of verbal harangue from Laura for my meanderings. When I cut the engine, Laura looked at the Airstream and then at me.

"You're taking me camping? Your turtle told you to take me camping?"

"My turtle has a first name. Tiresias. The least you could do is treat him like a human being and show some respect by using it. As for camping, look where you're at, Laura. I don't think the back alleys of Wichita are hot camping spots."

I explained to her how T-Bone Smith runs what's referred to politely as an escort service out of his Airstream and moves around to avoid confrontation with the law. I had brought him in to Bomber Jackson several times on bail violations, but I had also cut him some slack a few times and he owed me for it.

"You can't seriously believe the kids would be here?"

"Of course not. But T-Bone is street-smart, knows the business and he knows what's happening out there on the street. If anybody knows anything, he will have heard something about it."

She looked dubious as we stepped out of the truck and onto the gravel of the alley. Old elm trees branched out over the alley and offered a little relief from the heat.

T-Bone opened the door to the Airstream and descended down onto the gravel alley. He is a ruddy, rosy-faced man, tall and skinny, with extra wide shoulders, so exaggerated physically, that's where his nickname came from. I didn't know his real first name, and I doubted his last name was really Smith.

He strode toward us, and although he is highly educated with a Masters degree in linguistics, I had never heard him use anything but his smooth, soft-voiced street vernacular. How he wound up doing what he was doing for a living is anybody's guess.

"Ooohhh, baby," he said, in his usual silky voice while keeping his eyes on Laura. "You bring me some new meat, Jimmy? She be fine. Soooo, fine. Sublime addition to the corps."

Laura stared him in the eyes, kicked off her right shoe and then toed it to the side.

"Ooohhh, baby, that gives me a thrill. But not here, honey. Come inside before you start doing that act."

Ever so slowly and gently, she lifted her right, teal-clad leg, the silk rippling in the light breeze, into an Aikido position with her foot above her shoulder. Then, she extended her foot until it touched his chest and with a quick flex thumped him hard enough to jolt him back two steps.

It didn't seem to faze him. "Ooohhh, baby. What flex-i-bility. I have clients who will pay highly for that."

Still staring at him, she lowered her leg without saying anything.

"Okay. Okay. I get the message." He turned his attention to me. "What can I do ya for, Jimmy?"

"We need some information-"

"Whoa. I see nothing. I know nothing. You know me by now, Jimmy. That's how I operate and that's how I survive."

"Hear me out, T-Bone. You have the opportunity to be of service to all of Humanity. Something I know you aspire to."

"Yes Sir, I do have high ideals."

"Then maybe you can help us," said Laura.

"Ooohhh, baby. She speaks. That is even more impressive-"

Laura cut him off with one of her patented looks, and then resumed. "Recently a number of children were taken and we believe are being held for, or dealt off to the trafficking trade. We need to find them. Fast."

He held both hands up in front of himself, shoulder-high, palms toward us. "Ladies and Gentlemen, I do not travel in such company. I run a respectable business here."

"Yeah." Laura looked at the trailer. "Real respectable," she said. "How much respect do you think the ladies in that trailer have for themselves?"

"I treat my ladies-"

I cut him off this time. "You're missing the point, T-Bone. I've done you a few favors now and then. Now it's your turn to reciprocate."

Laura looked at me. "Reciprocate?"

"He's got an advanced degree in linguistics, Laura. Come on T-Bone. Info. Cough it up."

"Like I said. See nothing. Know nothing."

I was getting a little exasperated. I looked at the trailer. "Does Vice know where you are currently parked?"

"Jimmy. You wouldn't. You're not that low."

I kept staring at the trailer.

"Well, seeing as I do owe you a favor. But this squares us, right?"

"If the information is good."

"I do seem to remember hearing something. But, Jimmy, these are bad people. Really bad. If word gets out, it could be nasty for me. Great violence could be done to my personage. You gotta give me your word."

"Like you, Sir, I am a man of honor."

Laura rolled her eyes in disgust.

He looked around and began talking even softer than usual for him "What I hear is, and this is strictly off the record, I hear that traffickers moved in a few months ago. Got a base of operations and work a couple sides of the street. Locally, they're doing photographic work for the internet pedophile trade. When they're done, they ship some of them off to the underground movie industry and the rest go to Indonesia or the Far East for the street trade there."

"You have this kind of information about children and you didn't tell anyone?"

"I hear nothing. I see nothing. I survive."

Laura pressed him immediately. "Who is involved locally? Where can we find this base of operations, as you call it?"

"Sweetheart, if I possessed that kind of information, I would have sold it long ago."

I continued the press. "If you heard that much, there must have been some detail that would give us a start toward finding them. Even a lead to the source of the information. Anything would be helpful."

"All I know is that locally, there's some kind of photo-internet operation. International distribution, big money and really high-tech. That's it. That's all I know."

I stared at his Airstream. "And?"

"Oh, Jimmy. Why you doin' me like this?"

I kept the trailer stare up.

"Listen, you breathe a word of this about me on the street and I am a dead man. You understand?"

I nodded and stared.

"North of downtown," he said, "Somewhere in that No-Man's-Land industrial area. You know, out by the old stockyards where you got train tracks intersecting and old, empty cinderblock warehouses and rusty metal storage buildings and open fields of weeds in between. Empty semis parked for weeks at a time. They got some kind of operation there and it's so high tech they had to build a receiving or a sending tower or something, I don't know. That's it, Jimmy. That's all I know and that's the by-God truth."

As Laura and I drove off, my truck's tires crunching on the alley's gravel, I saw our informant in my rearview mirror, sitting on the step of his Airstream. He looked down, dejected, his wide T-bone shoulders hunched over, staring at a little patch of grass in the gravel.

"A real man of honor," said Laura. "Such high ideals, as he put it."

There wasn't much I could say to that. We rode in silence for a few minutes.

"Well," said Laura, "It looks like Tiresias gave you some bum information. So much for your prophetic turtle helping us."

"Au contraire, my dear. We have just learned a great deal."

"Other than an intense desire to scour my body clean with a Brillo pad, what have we got to show for that little disgusting encounter?"

"We'll soon find out. We are headed for No-Man's-Land."

10

"There it is," I said.

We sat in my pickup in an empty parking lot, if it could be called a parking lot.

"I could have had us here in half the time if you'd have let me drive today." Laura hated it when I made her ride with me. She looked around with a blank stare.

"There's nobody here. There's nothing here at all." Her look implied I had wasted the last hour of driving around.

"It's the only tower in the area. If T-Bone's information is correct, this has to be it."

"You trusted the word of a man with an advanced degree in linguistics who earns his living as a pimp selling female flesh, and this is what it got you. Nothing." She looked around at the open fields dotted with abandoned, rusty machinery and vehicles, the unused buildings scattered here and there, and the silent warehouses and grain silos next to railroad tracks. "He was right about one thing. This really is No-Man's-Land."

"If this is a dead-end, then those kids may as well be dead too."

Not willing to give up yet, I stepped down out of the truck on to the hot asphalt. The vast parking lot was nothing but a blacktop sea of cracks and buckled chunks, with weeds protruding everywhere. Nothing moved in the heat. The silence was eerie. The building next to the tower was a squat, square cinderblock structure, with a metal door and no windows. Laura got out and stood next to me, looking as despondent as I felt.

"Let's go, O'Reilly."

"Wait a minute. Listen."

"To what? There's nothing to listen to."

"Can't you hear it?"

We stood in the silent, empty void for what seemed like a long time.

"There's a faint hum," said Laura.

"An air conditioner. Look." I pointed, and on top of the building we could see the sun glint off of metal on a large industrial air conditioner that hummed a soft, steady cadence.

"Somebody uses this place for something. What better spot to disguise an internet pornography setup?" I said.

We walked up to the door and listened, but could hear nothing through the metal. I lightly twisted the handle. Locked. I got my B and E kit from the truck, then quickly and silently opened the door.

A blast of cold air hit us as we slid into a large, dimly lit room. When our eyes adjusted, we saw a wide, open room littered with equipment. One corner held tripods, cameras lined up on tables and various scenic backdrops. Next to it hung various bondage articles from simple handcuffs to an elaborate wooden stock. There were lines of computers and one long wall had shelf after shelf of computer discs. Then, on the opposing wall, thousands of pictures of children hung.

"These are disgusting," said Laura. "I think I'm going to be sick."

But just then, we heard a muffled noise from one corner and saw a tarp move. I pulled back the covering and a bound and gagged child lay beneath it.

"Esteban. It's Esteban," said Laura.

He slid back, wide eyed with fear, as we cut the plastic cuffs and undid his gag.

"¿Donde está Esperanza?" I asked about his sister. His terrified eyes darted to a door that was concealed by a partition. I looked at Laura. She motioned me to go ahead while she put her arm around Esteban and comforted him.

I put one hand around my Ruger and withdrew it from its pocket holster, and in one swift motion turned the door handle and entered the next room, Ruger poised for fire. Two men turned in surprise and we stared at each other, frozen. Both were Asian, apparently Japanese. A shirtless one had intricate tattoos over his entire torso, up over his shoulders and down his arms into the wrists and the back of his hands. The fully clothed one had tattoos sprouting from beneath his shirt in every conceivable direction. They stood in front of an open back door.

Shirtless blinked first, and when his eyes flicked left and mine followed, both men bolted out the door and into the sunlight.

I balked, because to the left, where he looked, was a pen crowded with imprisoned children.

"Laura," I yelled. "In here now." Then I shot through the door into sunlight by myself. But a van that had been parked and concealed behind the building raced off, bouncing over chunks of buckled blacktop in the parking lot. I was torn between going back to the children and pursuing the van. My indecision cost me. By the time I came around to the front of the building to my truck, they were gone.

Back inside, Laura had already called it in on her cell, and then pulled the pin on the makeshift lock for the pen, releasing the terrified kids.

Within two minutes, we heard the sirens.

*****

Two hours later Laura and I sat in a large room at City Hall on North Main. It was bustling with locals, Immigration, interpreters, reps from the National Center for Missing and Exploited Children and just about every other agency you could think of.

Little Julio, Elena, Esteban and Esperanza were safe, as well as all the other little ones, twelve total, who had been involved, at least by the children's account. The kids had been parceled out to smaller rooms where they met with counselors, and preparations were being made for medical checks.

Laura and I, done with our numerous interviews and interrogations, readied ourselves to leave when Charlie waltzed in, having descended from sixth floor Homicide above us. She's tall, and her dark hair framed her sturdy face as she marched toward us in her brown uniform and shiny black belt with all the bells and whistles of her profession attached.

"You're a little out of your bailiwick, aren't you?" I said. "Nice of you to descend from your sixth floor perch."

"Heard you were in the neighborhood and wondered why you hadn't come up to see me. Have I lost favor?" She smiled a wicked smile at Laura, but she knows Laura and I are friends and nothing more.

"I've been a little indisposed."

"So I've heard. Leave it to you to wind up involved in something like this."

"Hey, you're the one responsible. Remember the Mrs. Gonzalez referral?"

She looked away for a moment. "Oh, yeah. Look, if those kids are all safe now, you need to cut out. This is turning into nasty business. Our computer guy says that whole electronic set up you stumbled on not only used passwords, they had encrypted files, evidence-eliminator software and peer-to-peer networks in order to evade authorities."

"What does that mean?" said Laura.

"It means it was one hell of a sophisticated operation and will take months to sort out. On top of that, it looks like the Yakuza is involved and you don't want to have anything to do if they're around."

Laura and I looked at one another. "What's a Yakuza?" I said.

"It's not a what. It's a who. The Japanese Mafia. They have no regard for anyone but they're own, and you can see that from what they planned on doing with those kids."

"Japanese Mafia? I didn't even know there was such a thing. Do the Italians know about them?"

"I would have pegged you to have watched some of the Yakuza movies that are out there. You're the one hooked on old revenge flicks, like Charles Bronson and Steven Segal. Right up your alley. Anyway, time to leave the rough stuff for the big boys, Bruiser." She was referring to my old nickname, Bruiser the Cruiser, from when I boxed Cruiserweight class on the force.

I ignored the dig, but Laura suppressed a laugh, and as we turned to leave and I headed out to retrieve my Ruger from Security, Charlie called out after us.

"By the way O'Reilly. Caught your performance on the news the other night. Very impressive. I haven't heard such great in-depth tit analysis in a long time. Are you doing an ass appraisal on your next show? You plan on hosting your own talk show, or just going to be a regular guest commentator for sexist body-part analysis on CNN?"

Laura cut loose with a snort and a loud laugh as I hustled her out the door.

*****

Later that evening, I sat in my bungalow and sipped a glass of Dutch Henry Terrier Station red, thinking through all that had happened in the last few days. I tried to sort it all out and make some sense of it all. My musings were interrupted by a knock at the door. When I opened up, Inez Gonzalez looked up at me. I ushered her in and we sat facing one another in my living room.

"I am sorry to have come so late, but I want to thank you, Mr. O'Reilly. Both you and your kind friend, Miss Bascome. Little Julio and Elena are safe. If it weren't for the two of you, they would not be here today."

"That's quite alright, Mrs. Gonzalez," I said.

"I don't know what will happen at the end, but for now, they are with me. I only hope they can stay here. I do not know what the law will say."

"I don't either." I shrugged. I truly didn't have a clue as to what all the agencies would declare in the end.

"Here." She fished in her purse and pulled out a wad of bills. "Now, I pay you."

"Oh no. Wait just a minute. Your sister-in-law has not been found and we don't know what's happened to her. You wait until all this has been resolved."

"You are a good man, Mr. O'Reilly. Thank you for all that you are doing."

After she left, I questioned her "good man" analysis as I regretted implying that I would continue searching. But I was exhausted, and fell asleep on my couch, fully clothed, and unaware of the events yet to come.

Instead, I dreamed about an old Irish myth my grandfather, James O'Reilly, told me when I was little, or as he put it, "When you were a wee one." He was a shanachie, a story teller versed in the old myths, and this was a tale of childhood innocence called The Children of

Lir, but it always filled me with fear. Somehow, as a little boy, I thought it could happen to me. This is how he told it:

In ancient Ireland, Lir's wife bears him four children, a son and a daughter who are twins, and two sons who are also twins. However, she dies while giving birth to the two sons. Her sister agrees to marry Lir and lovingly care for the children, which she initially does. But when she becomes childless herself, she transforms into the evil stepmother, jealous of the children, and takes revenge upon them.

Taking them on a journey far away, she pushes them into a lake and uses a druid's wand to magically turn them into images of beautiful white swans. The curse is to last for nine hundred years, during which they are to retain their full powers of human speech and recognition, as well as the gift of beautiful song.

So, for nine centuries, they wander the waterways of Ireland, singing their story in glorious melody to the world, but also seeing the devastation that time wrought, the abandonment and decay of their home and death of their father, and knowing that all their loss will greet them when they eventually come back as humans. Their sorrow is so immense...

I woke from the dream in a night sweat, breathing heavily and gasping for breath. As I sat on the edge of the couch, my chest heaving, I thought of Julio and Elena and Esteban and Esperanza, and how their images were almost captured and transformed for all eternity, and how their innocence was so close to being lost forever.

I picked up the volume of Irish poetry and reread the MacDonagh poem, but this time two new lines jumped out at me.

A child sang welcomes of the gate of Light-
Welcome to the peace of perfect night

I thought about all four children. All four children of Lir, singing their song to the world. All four children of the many rescued yesterday, and wondered what peace they might be having of a perfect night tonight. I hoped it was a gentle one.

11

By the time the sun came up it was already hot. I decided to forgo my planned section run and weight workout, and instead walked into town for coffee and breakfast at Latte Dottie's on Commercial Street.

But as soon as I was out my front door, wide-brimmed William, now individually filling in all the gash marks from his dandelion massacre, hollered over to me.

"Did the lady in the blue convertible find you?" he said.

"Blue convertible? Who might that be, William?"

"Don 't know, but she came a callin' yesterday. Pretty young thing. I say, you got more of them pretty young things after you than I can shake a stick at."

"Yeah, they're busting my door down," I said, with a fairly weary sarcasm in my voice. "Thanks for letting me know." His description didn't ring a bell and I started off for Dottie's.

"When you gonna pick one and settle down? A handsome widow-man like you ought to have a permanent lady-fixture in the house."

"As soon as I reach puberty," I said. I didn't correct his misuse of widow, and I didn't wait for a reaction and headed immediately to Dottie's diner.

Latte Dottie's moniker was an oxymoron, because you couldn't get latte there. She only served black coffee.

Strong black coffee, and she became offended if you asked for anything else, including cream or sugar.

Dottie's was also the point of exchange for town gossip, so any news I'd missed out on I could be sure to get caught up on. When I walked in I got a bonus, because Alex sat at the counter, so I plopped myself down next to him.

"What's shakin'?" I asked.

"Jimmy. Just the man I need to see. Fill me in on the going's-on you was involved in yesterday."

Dottie came out from the back to take my order. She's got steel gray eyes that can bore a hole right through you with one of her stares. I started to make my usual joke anyway of asking for a latte, but she cut me short in her harsh, guttural voice.

"Don't even think of it, Jimmy, or you'll be eating this menu for your breakfast." She brandished a plastic covered menu in my face.

"I love you, too," I said. "Just give me my usual, Dottie."

"That's better." And she toddled off into the back.

After I told Alex about the previous day's events, I pumped him for information.

"What's the news on the home front? You find anything out about the body Jack brought us in on out by Dale's farm?"

"Fingerprints come back. I mean, for the ones he still had. They belong to a man by the name of Robert Townsend. He's an over-the-road hauler, independent owner-operator. Works out of San Antonio."

"Was he the driver of that death truck?"

"He might of been, but that wasn't his rig. His rig's been found down in Oklahoma across the Kansas line at a truck stop off of I-35."

"What about that key in his pocket?"

"We tried it on that lock you bolt-cut from the truck's rear doors. Didn't fit. Course, the cab was gone, so we couldn't check that. Looks like it could be one of those locker keys, like you find at truck stops and bus stations, but no leads so far."

Dottie came in with my breakfast and coffee.

"Well, gotta scoot, Jimmy. Talk to you later."

After Alex left, Dottie came over with one of her wry smiles on her face.

"What do you know that you aren't telling me, Dottie?"

"I know you're probably glad them newshounds have mostly packed up and left town. Not bothering you anymore."

The sensationalism of the incident had worn off, and Chisholm was no longer the hot news item of the day.

"Yes, I am. I guess the town's economy got a boost from all that, but we're better off and a lot quieter since they're gone."

"You missed out. That blonde reporter was hot to find you."

Geeze, I thought. Everyone's playing matchmaker. "I meant, anything of real importance you aren't telling me?"

"Just that Lon Claymore's been back in these parts. Scouting around. Rumor is he's looking for land. Going to build something. Something big. Now that'll do miracles for our economy."

With Dottie's new observations and information, I walked back home, mentally ticking off the computer research items I needed to do today to prepare for some skip trace jobs for Bomber Jackson.

As I walked up Fourth Street toward my house, I stopped short. A blue convertible sat in my drive, top down. William had gone inside, but I could see him peeking out from behind some window curtains, observing.

I walked up to the passenger side door and looked down at Charlene Claymore sitting in her blue convertible. Her seat reclined and her slim body lay back in it with her eyes closed. She wore a yellow sundress hiked up above her thighs, and her brunette hair had been tossed by the wind from driving. Her cheeks were flushed, and when she opened her eyes she batted her eyelashes at me.

"Why Jimmy O'Reilly," she said, looking up at me. "Fancy meeting you here."

"What can I do for you, Mrs. Claymore?"

"Please, don't be so formal, Jimmy. I may call you that, mayn't I?"

I looked down and there was a six pack of Bud on the front passenger seat, one bottle empty, and an open bottle of Jack Daniels next to a cup in the center caddy.

"It's a little early in the day for boilermakers, isn't it?" I said.

"Just jumpstarting my day. That's all. I was wondering if you might want to take a spin with me. It's a lovely day for a drive in the country, don't you think?"

"I'm afraid we would be in violation of the open container law," I said, looking at the cup, beer and liquor bottles.

"Oh, come on, Jimmy. Don't be an old stick-in-the-mud. Let's have a little fun, you and me."

"What would your husband say?"

"My so-called husband has no interest in what I do. He's much too concerned with his precious political career. That, and his business. He seems obsessed with building things and labor contracts and how to pay the help."

"Thank you for your offer Mrs. Claymore, but I have to get to work myself right now. Have a good day." I turned and walked up my front steps.

"Foo on you," she yelled. She started the car, backed out, and gunned the engine as she peeled out down the street.

A half hour later as I sat at my computer researching skip trace jobs, gears meshed in my brain and something clicked. Labor contracts and paying the help, she had said, and I suddenly began wondering what connection Lon Claymore might have, if any, to the importation of undocumented workers.

I began a search engine hunt for anything related to his family business and was amazed at what popped up. Claymore Oil had become a successful family business, no doubt, but I now saw so much more. By following link after link, some of them hidden and obscure, I found the company had become vertically integrated, and it looked as if there wasn't a great deal of transparency about it either. The information was about as covert and inaccessible as it could be.

Instead of just a family oil company, they were now involved in pipeline manufacturing, materials acquisition, trucking and transportation, and even cattle and large tracts of grazing land. No wonder he could afford a house with a solarium.

This whole new perspective put an additional spin on Charlene Claymore's mention of labor contracts and paying the help. Any one of these levels of reinvented Claymore Oil Company might benefit greatly from different aspects of the illegal alien trade.

I had just started thinking about where to begin with this massive opportunity when the phone rang. It was Laura.

"O'Reilly, I want to introduce you to someone."

"Okay," I said. "And this is regarding?"

"Look. The kids are safe. For now, at least. We'll have to see what happens with the system. But I am not going to let go of the other end of it. The women. I'm not going to let the women be swept under the rug, and I'm not going to let you let go either."

Here was Laura's social consciousness raising it's lovely head again. "We don't even know if there are women. And we certainly don't know where to start."

"We know there's Maria, and from what you told me about the inside of that trailer and what you saw there, we know there are probably more."

"Granted, but I repeat. We don't know where to start."

"That is why I am introducing you to someone. It's our starting point."

"Okay," I said, resigned to the fact and to Laura's obsessive nature with justice. "How about tomorrow morning?"

"How about in two minutes? I'm on my way now, just outside of Chisholm. I'll see you in a jiffy. Ta-ta."

That's Laura for you.

12

Laura's red Vette sped west out of Chisholm.

"If I would have let you drive, this trip would take a week and a half instead if a few hours."

Laura's eyes stayed on the road, but I knew there was fire in them. She hated riding in my truck because of how slow I drive, relative to her, that is. And she hated following me, always tailgating and gunning her engine to let me know. So when she arrived at my place, she insisted on driving. At least the top was on and we had air conditioning.

"You must be taking me somewhere rustic." I looked at her designer jeans, high-end denim shirt and signed red kerchief around her neck. That was about as rustic as Laura could get with her wardrobe.

"The country air will do you good."

"So, just who is this someone you felt you had to introduce me to, and had to do so immediately?"

"Akira Sato. He's a Yamabushi."

After a few moments of silence, I said, "I'm not going to ask about the name part. But I gotta know. What's a Yamabushi?"

"He's a Japanese mountain ascetic. You know, a person that lives alone in the mountains, like a hermit, for peace and introspection. Truth seekers. Spiritual mountain guides. Priests and monks. In the old days in Japan they were the warrior monks."

"As improbable as it may seem, I get it all, except for the mountain part. I hate to break the news to you, Laura. Except for Mt. Sunflower, which doesn't count because it's not really a mountain, there are no mountains in Kansas."

"We got big hills."

"True. But how does that qualify for this Yamabushwacker, or whatever you call him that's supposed to be a monk and live in the mountains and be a spiritual mountain guide?"

"Yamabushi. We're speaking figuratively. Think of it this way. You can build mountains around yourself, figuratively, anywhere in the world. In your mind. You could be in the middle of Times Square and have mountains around you."

"Okay." I wasn't convinced, but I was playing along.

"I met Akira through my Aikido instructor. She told me it was time for me to learn Reiki, you know, the hands-on healing system, and that this Akira Sato, a Reiki Master, would be my teacher. So, he gave me my level one instruction and attunement about a year ago."

We had been driving for some time and were traveling through flat, open prairie land. "You're taking me out in the middle of no-where to get hands-on healing from a Reiki Master?"

"You could probably use it, but no, Akira Sato is our possible link to the missing women."

Now I was really stumped. How could a Japanese man who intentionally isolates himself from the rest of the world, mountains or not, know anything about kidnapped Hispanic illegal alien women? It made absolutely no sense. I was about to ask Laura when she jerked the car off onto the shoulder of the two-lane and came to a screeching halt.

"Get out."

"We're there?"

"No, but there's something you need to see."

Off on the side of the road was a State historical marker. We stood reading about the site where the town of Runnymede once thrived in the eighteen hundreds. Now it was just bare prairie.

"Well, I do have to thank you, Laura. I have never been here before."

Runnymede was the town where my great-great grandparents, Mark and Bridget O'Reilly immigrated to from Cork, Ireland and set up shop teaching English nobles how to farm and ranch. It was probably the first-ever dude ranch.

As Laura and I sped off toward the Yamabushi's hideout, wherever it was, I sat riding shotgun thinking about my ancestors. Their dude ranch enterprise eventually collapsed, and he wound up as an abolitionist fighting on the side of the Freestaters. The O'Reilly's fled violence in Ireland and came to violence on the plains. Violence is imbued in my family and I am no exception. One continuous cycle that has been difficult for me to live with, and impossible to break. From my wife's murder to my everyday job.

As we traveled west and south, more and more oil wells began populating the landscape, and trucks and rigs dotted the fields. A sight you wouldn't have seen a few years ago. Rig workers and drillers labored in the heat of the day.

The landscape began changing, and we were now traveling through rolling hills. After we passed through the tiny town of Zenda, and I facetiously wondered how many prisoners they might have there, we saw the sharp dividing line between the Wellington Lowlands of the east and the Red Hills on the west. A high escarpment stretched before us, separating the two geographical areas, and we wound up and through it on some back dirt road in the middle of the Cimarron Breaks.

"See," she said. "Mountains."

"Try selling that concept to someone from Colorado," I said. "The Rockies never looked so good."

She slowed down and when she found what she was looking for, turned off the narrow dirt road onto a narrower winding dirt drive. After cresting a hill, the drive ended, so she parked and we started walking.

Despite my facetious comment about her wardrobe earlier, she had indeed dressed for the terrain. Her coordinated jeans outfit, along with a wild rhinestone studded belt and hiking boots, served her well as we walked a trail for about a quarter of a mile.

Then, right there before us in the hot afternoon sun, on the top of a red dirt mesa, a man stood. Naked. Totally and completely naked.

His back was toward us, and his muscular shoulders and tapered torso and bare buttocks all glistened under the running water of a man-made waterfall.

Laura whispered to me. "He's purifying himself."

"Good," I whispered back. "I like naked bodies that are pure. Although I prefer female naked pure bodies."

"It's a ritual," she whispered.

The naked body had not yet turned around when a rich baritone voice sounded out from it. "Laura-san. Welcome. Whom have you brought with you to see me?"

"How did he know we were here, and how did he know it's you?" I whispered. But before she could answer, he spoke again.

"No matter. Sit. I will return."

His bare body left and entered a primitive shack that could not have had running water or sanitary devices. Laura and I sat on a log near the so-called waterfall.

"He just knows," said Laura. "He's got an uncanny ability to be totally aware of all that's going on around him."

"What's this san stuff? Laura-san."

"It's just a sign of respect."

Next to the log where we sat were racks with carved wooden objects on them. Laura saw me looking.

"Those are Aikido staffs and walking sticks. He carves them and then lets them cure in the sun."

Indeed, each staff was quite plain, except for one or two bands of carvings that included animals, human faces and designs, all beautiful and intricate.

A short while later, he emerged from the shack dressed in some kind of a costume. He wore white, full breeches that flared out angularly and then were tucked into leggings bound with black cloth around the calves. He had a white angular jacket with vast pleated sleeves. Four orange pom-poms hung around his neck and a purple bungee cord looking thing with bells on the end looped through a belt. An Aikido staff hung across his back and some kind of a giant conch shell hung at his waist. He held a walking staff in one hand with six metal rings attached. He walked with wooden sandals on his feet.

"If this is a costume party," I whispered to Laura, "I didn't get the memo. I'm underdressed." Laura pulled me up to stand before him.

He came forward and stood before us on this flat-topped rugged mesa, with the red iron oxide rust of the sandstone and shale contrasting sharply with his stark white clothing. The washed-out gullies of the Cimarron Breaks flowed in the background. I thought I was in an old "Seven Samurai" movie.

"Welcome, Laura-san." He bowed slightly.

"Sato-sensei. This is my friend, Jimmy-san." She bowed slightly and he returned it.

Jimmy-san? I thought. It sounds like I'm in a Looney Tunes cartoon.

"Welcome, Jimmy-san. Is your pain great?" He said, looking at me.

I looked at him, believing he was older than me, yet thinking he actually looked younger. He seemed timeless. I laughed. "No," I said. "I don't have any pain."

"Your chest and your side. You have been injured. Perhaps beaten."

I thought about the two-by-four blow I'd taken from the flannel-shirted, non-sweating guy in the shed, and it did still hurt. Quite a bit. "How does he know about that?" I said to Laura.

He stepped up to me and placed both hands on my solar plexus, directly over where I'd taken the blow. Immediately, his hands and my gut and chest heated up. We're talking hot. Really hot. Then, after a few silent minutes, all the pain subsided and I was able to take easy, full breaths with no sharp, jabbing stabs in my side.

He removed his hands and sat down in front of us on the ground, seiza style, with his legs tucked up under him and indicated for us to sit.

"How'd you do that thing with your hands?" I said, taking a deep, full breath and sitting.

"No matter. You are better now."

"That's Reiki," said Laura. "I told you he is a Reiki Master."

"With what may I help you?" He said, again looking directly at me.

His grammar was impeccable and there was no trace of any accent, although his syntax and word choice sometimes seemed a little awkward.

"How do you know we need help?" I said.

He covered his mouth, laughed a giggly little laugh, and then said to Laura, "Your friend is funny. Explain the problem to me and I will determine a course of action."

Laura told him all that had happened, and when she finished he looked out over the red mesa top at the far horizon for a long time.

"This is bad business," he said. "I will see you tomorrow." Then he got up and went into his shack.

*****

Laura drove in silence and I sat in silence on the way back to Chisholm. Finally, I could contain my frustration no longer.

"That's it?" I said. "You brought me out in the middle of the desolate Cimarron Breaks for that?"

"He said he'll see you tomorrow."

"I'm not going back."

"No, you're not. He'll be coming to you."

"How? He has no visible means of transportation. What does he do, flap his white robed wings and fly? And I'm not sitting around my house waiting for him, either."

"You don't have to. Do whatever you're going to do tomorrow and he'll find you."

I threw up my hands in exasperation and then shut up.

*****

My front door was open.

Janie sat on my terrace reading from my Irish poets' book as Laura and I looked out through the open French doors at her. She was oblivious to our presence, completely absorbed.

"She is quite the young lady, isn't she?" I said.

"For a fourteen year old who's been through what she's been though. Yes."

Out beyond her in the yard, W.B., her yellow lab, lay on the grass, nose to nose with Tiresias.

She looked up and acknowledged our presence, squinting at us. "Hello, Mr. O. Hi, Laura."

"Hi, Janie." I squinted back. "Everything okay here?"

"Yes, Sir. I got your stone turtle collection dusted. And all your herbs have been watered. The basil was really dry. And Tiresias wandered up and seemed to be looking for you. I don't know if he's just lonely, or if he's got something to tell you. But I brought W.B. over to keep him company."

"Thanks, Janie. You're the best."

"Looks like they're getting along famously," said Laura.

"Yeah. I think they like each other. Volleyball practice got out early today, so I just came right over and took care of things."

"What are you reading?"

"One of my favorites. I like to reread that Yeats poem, 'The Lake Isle of Innisfree.' You know the line, 'And I shall have some peace there, for peace comes dropping slow.' That's what I feel like when I sit on your terrace with all the herbs and Tiresias and W.B. It's just so peaceful here."

"Well, thank you, Janie. It's nice of you to say so." I caught myself squinting at her for no apparent reason.

*****

After Laura left and drove Janie and W.B. home, I sat on the bench in my terrace thinking how right Janie was. It did feel peaceful here. It's funny how you get so used to your surroundings that you don't really appreciate them for what they are.

I looked out and Ty's head stretched out of his shell, basking in the sun. I sat back and let the warm, still peace "drop slow" over me, too, even if it was only a temporary feeling.

13

I was up a blind alley. Literally. Lost.

I'd left for Wichita early the next morning on a skip trace job, parked my truck, and walked to the address I was looking for. Except that it didn't exist. I rounded the next corner, walked down the alley to look from the back, and here I stood facing a brick wall at its dead-end.

I know the streets of Wichita well, all the ins and outs of how to get where, and all the short cuts. This didn't make sense. I had that brief feeling of panic that hits when you are not only lost, but completely disoriented.

I turned around to head back out of the alley and nearly jumped out of my skin.

"What the hell are you doing here?" I yelled.

Akira Sato stood directly in front of me, not more than a foot away, face to face with me.

"You scared the living daylights out of me," I said, catching my breath.

"I told you I would see you today," he said, his voice impassive.

"You scare a guy like that and don't even offer an apology?"

"I'm sorry. Not sorry that you think I frightened you. I am only sorry you have allowed fear to enter you."

Oh, great. Just what I needed. A philosopher. "You scared the shit out of me."

He sniffed the air. "It doesn't smell like it."

Double-great. A standup comic, too. "What are you doing here, ah... What do I call you anyway? Akira? Mister Sato-san, or sensei? What do you go by?"

"Whatever you want to call me. I call you Jimmy-san."

Triple-great. I'm back in that Looney Tunes cartoon again. I expected Daffy, Bugs or Yosemite Sam to pop up at any moment. At least he wasn't in his puffy white cartoon costume with pom-poms. He was dressed in jeans, a navy tee and sneakers, the only accessory being his Aikido stick slung over his back.

"Where's your costume, Akira-san?" I figured if he was going to san me, I'd san him right back.

"I try to dress for the occasion, Jimmy-san." He smiled.

It looked as if we were going to spend the morning trying to out-san each other. "Look, I don't even know how you got here, but I've got work to do. So, if you'll excuse me."

"You come with me now." He turned and walked toward the daylight at the front of the alley, leaving me standing in shadow and staring after him.

I called out to him. "Hey. I have a skip trace job to do and I have to get back and do computer research on..." I trailed off and then found myself actually following him, and I didn't even know why. Back out on the street, I didn't see my truck anywhere and everything still looked unfamiliar.

He wasn't walking fast, yet I found myself having trouble keeping up. I looked around and didn't recognize anything. It was as if I was in a strange city I had never visited before.

"Where are you taking me?" I said, lengthening my stride to keep up.

"I'm not taking you. You are following. If you come, I want you to meet my son." He looked straight ahead as we talked.

"Your son? I thought you were a monk or something."

"I am. I'm a Tendai priest. Unlike many Christian priests, some of us take wives and have children. I have done both."

We must have walked for ten minutes with no landmarks I recognized, when he finally stopped in front of an ordinary one story office building. The front windows were curtained and the glass door opaque, with barely visible lettering that read: EASTERN IMPORT COMPANY.

He finally turned and looked at me. "Come in. This is where my son works."

I followed him in to a small front room with a desk and several racks of papers that looked like blank invoices. Nobody was there. The one desk was completely clear, nothing on its top. No phone existed. Through a door at the back of the room I saw a small empty warehouse. There were a few boxes in one corner of the office and I walked over to look in one of them as he called out for his son.

"Toshi."

The open box looked like it contained cheap touristy trinkets. Everything about the place hinted at a phony setup. A front for something illegal. I was about to lift one of the trinkets out of its box when his son entered the room.

"Hello, Father."

"This is my son, Toshi," Akira said.

But when I turned around, the man standing across the room looked back at me with as much surprise as I'm sure I registered right back at him.

It was the shirtless tattooed man, now fully clothed, who had sped away in a van from the cinderblock building with the children.

Akira looked back and forth at the two of us, perplexed, until Toshi made the first move, whirled, and sped out the door he'd entered. I bolted after him but he was out through a back door, and when I exited and looked both ways, he was gone. Vanished. It was as if he had never been there. That's twice he'd pulled that maneuver on me.

*****

"Tell me about it."

A short time later, Akira and I sat on an embankment in a shaded grassy open area between two groups of cottonwoods, and looked out over the Arkansas River. At least I knew where I was now. We passed my truck on the way, and over the treetops I could see the top of the Keeper of the Plains statue from where we sat. I'd gotten my bearings back. I was in the real world again.

"Oh. I have no face," he said.

"What?"

"I have no face. I am so ashamed," he said.

"Of what?"

"The dishonor my son has brought us."

"You'd better start at the beginning," I said.

He stared off toward the river and was silent for a long time. Then he said, "My wife and I came here several years ago because of our son. Toshi came to the United States to study. At least that is what we thought. We found out later he had become involved with the Yakuza."

There's that name again, I thought. "The Japanese Mafia?" I said.

"If you want to call it that. Yes. The Yakuza. Slowly, little by little, we brought him back to us and away

84

from the life of crime. He was able to separate himself from that life and he took a job with the import company. Or so we thought. Now, I have learned differently. I am so ashamed."

We sat in silence for awhile. I was about ready to tell him it was time we go report what had happened, when he reached out and put one hand over my heart. It heated up, just like the other time he did it.

"I don't know what this Reiki thing is or what you do or how you do it, but that injury is all healed. You fixed it yesterday."

"This is for a different injury. This is for your heart. You have had a great loss that you carry in your heart, and you must release the hurt."

Suddenly, I was overcome with the soft fragrance of pine needles, the scent of my wife's hair the night she died. A scent that always comforted me. Her hair that brushed against my face that night as she kissed me when she left the house. Hair the color of ripe wheat. I don't know how he could have known about my wife's death, but it didn't matter.

"Look, that was years ago. I've gotten over it."

"No. You still carry it with you. If you do not release it, it will be your undoing."

I sat thinking about Sondra's murder and how I dealt with it all these years. It was still so much a mystery to me, even though I felt I had moved on. When Akira removed his hand and the heat subsided, suddenly I felt much lighter.

"Okay, Mr. Know-It-All. Explain something else to me," I said. "The entire time we just spent together, from when I turned around and you were standing there in that alley, until we left the import company, I had no idea where I was. Then suddenly, the landmarks were familiar again. I know this city inside and out. What was going on?"

"You had entered my world. The world that contains the secret of being here, and not being here."

"That's a little over my head."

"Just remember, wherever you go, you meet yourself."

"Huh?"

"The city you know inside and out, as you put it, is the city you created. The city you were in for that brief period of time is the city I created."

"I'm not getting it, Akira."

"No matter. You will. Now we will go." He stood up. "You will take me in the city you have created to the local authorities. As much shame as I have, all of this must be told."

"That," I said, "I understand perfectly. And that's one thing you're right about."

*****

Late that afternoon, I sat in a lawn chair on the spillway of Wiley's pond along with my SureShot bucket of stink bait, casting out for catfish. It didn't matter if the bobber never bobbed. If I caught anything it was always catch-and-release anyway. This was just my method of thinking things through.

I figured it was high time to do just that. See if I could make sense of all the different things that had happened and bring some order to it all. Mainly, just try to figure out what to do next. If anything at all.

It was hot, dry and dusty, and I let the sun pound my brain to see what kind of information might bake out of it.

The Feds and KBI and the locals were all collaborating on the deaths of the men in the trailer. At least as much as all those agencies had the ability to collaborate. The man who took me hostage and whacked me with the two-by-four was, at this point, a dead-end. I had nothing to go on there. The authorities might come up with something from the cinderblock building where the kids were, but the whole Yakuza thing was a blank to me. Although, Akira said "he would see me" again. Whatever that meant, and whatever promise that might hold.

Lon Claymore, on the other hand, offered a glimmer of hope. That avenue, at least had possibilities. Rumors were that he wanted to buy land. Rumors were that he was going to build something big. His wife said his only interests were politics, business and labor. Add all that up along with the fact that I'd never trusted the guy and I'd never liked him, and I sensed that something sure seemed out of kilter.

I figured I needed some face-time with Lon.

14

I'd spent fifteen long, frustrating minutes pushing the buzzer, announcing myself and making requests into the speaker at Lon Claymore's gated entrance with no one responding. I'd waved and hollered at gardeners and maintenance workers, and shouted at a pool boy inside the gates. All to no avail. I was getting really pissed. I considered climbing over the iron work when a truck pulled up.

The driver announced himself into the speaker and the gates immediately swung open. Just goes to show you, it's all in who you know and how important you are.

I jumped into my pickup and was on his tail and through the gates before they could close, and I sped around him like a jackrabbit out in front of a coyote, and coasted up to the front door ahead of him. The company logo on the side of his truck read Simpson Drilling Company, Ardmore, OK, with a bright yellow sun behind a silhouette of an oil derrick for a logo.

Lon Claymore sauntered down his front steps, dressed in khakis and a powder-blue polo, waving and smiling at me, his dough-face, pasty and puffed out.

"Jimmy. What a pleasure. And an unexpected one at that." He didn't extend his hand.

"Baxter has a way of showing up unexpectedly at my place, so I thought I would repay the kindness," I said, putting on my own silly little Irish grin.

"You might call ahead the next time. As you can see, I have other commitments at the moment." He gestured to the man getting out of the truck.

"I won't take more than a few minutes of your time, Lon."

"I wish I could, Jimmy, but I'm on a really tight schedule this morning. You know how it is."

As the man approached us, I said in voice loud enough for him to hear, "This concerns the resolution of those illegal immigrants' deaths and what might have happened to some who are still alive. Surely, your constituents would want to know the details of-"

"Just a minute, Jimmy." He cut me off and turned to the man who had gotten out of the Simpson Drilling Company truck. "Mr. Simpson, go on in and wait for me in the solarium. I'll be there shortly."

Mr. Simpson walked through the front door and headed straight for the solarium. He obviously knew where he was going.

Lon took me by the arm and guided me down a gravel path, out of earshot of workers. "I thought we had an understanding that you weren't going to pursue this incident any further, but leave it up to the authorities to resolve it."

"Understanding? The only thing I understand," I said, freeing my arm, "is that twenty-seven men are dead. Twelve children have been put through Hell, and an unknown number of women are missing." I felt my trapezius tightening and a corded knot was forming in my neck.

"It is unfortunate," he said.

"Unfortunate? It's an outrage and it's social injustice." A full blown headache was imminent. I started flexing my jaw.

"These are, after all, illegals. They have broken the law of the land and they are not entitled to the protection of our judicial system."

Suddenly, I just blurted it out. The thought that had been nagging at me for some time. "I think you had something to do with it. You're responsible for these deaths. You are involved and connected. Furthermore-"

"Stop right there." He held up both hands facing toward me. "You're out of bounds, Jimmy. Way out of bounds."

I lost control and unloaded on him, spewing it all out. "What are you buying up land for around here? What's this big thing everyone says you're going to build? How much labor do you need to do it and where are you going to get it all from? If you had anything to do with bringing those illegals in-"

"If you go any farther with this, I will slap a libel suit on you so big it'll take the rest of your life to get out from under it. It's sad it's come to this, Jimmy, after all these years. Now it's time for you to leave."

"Speaking of bringing in labor from places unknown, what are you bringing in a drilling company from out of state for?" I nodded toward the truck from Ardmore, Oklahoma.

He pulled some kind of a communication device from his hip pocket and spoke into it. "Baxter."

"Yes, Sir," it crackled back with static.

"I need you to come escort someone off the premises. We're on the side walkway near the rose garden."

"Yes, Sir. Be right there."

"Tell Baxter to forget it," I said. "I'm out of here."
If I saw Baxter I'd probably attack him and throttle his throat. Add assault to the libel charge.

When I drove up to the gate, it miraculously opened and let me exit. Suddenly I was important enough for gate action. No trouble leaving, I thought. Only getting in.

Way to go O'Reilly. You not only managed to piss the guy off, you came away with nothing. Zip. Zero. Zilch. That's me. The king of Zs.

15

I sat in Dottie's nursing an iced coffee. Iced coffee was about the only concession Dottie made beyond the house specialty. Java black, no exceptions.

"Why are your ears red?" she said, her voice dry and flat. "They match your hair."

I ignored her, took another sip and thought about how beautiful the morning was. It was the first morning with mild temperatures and a cool breeze, but my encounter with Lon Claymore had prevented me from enjoying it. I flexed my jaw and rotated my neck, trying to free up the knotted cord and my tight trapezius. It didn't help. A banded ache spread across my forehead.

Why did I always let Cretans like Lon get to me? I always walked away a casualty and never gained the upper hand. Yet it seemed like I couldn't help myself when confronted with people who regarded anyone other than themselves as unworthy and subhuman. How did these people operate like they were the upper end of the food chain, devouring everything they thought existed below them?

Now, I had nowhere to go. Another dead-end.

I went home, pumped iron for half an hour and then ran a section run, trying to sweat out the corded knot and headache that dogged me. It was good to pass by more combines rolling through the field corn, at least one sign of life going on.

I was deep into the run, sweating and breathing heavily, when I noticed a work truck out in the middle of a field. I couldn't read the lettering, but it had the same bright yellow sun logo on it that the Simpson Drilling truck had on it at Lon Claymore's place. Then, something clicked and I remembered the vehicles out in the oil fields on the way to Akira's place in the Cimarron Breaks.

They all had that same bright yellow sun logo. It burned in my mind like a flame that couldn't be put out. I knew there had to be some connection, some thread that ran through all of this, but I just couldn't put it all together.

On a hunch, after I showered, I went in town to see Alex. Trucks seemed to be a common denominator, so I thought I'd pump him for information. He sat hunched over his desk reading some reports, probably wishing he was drinking a beer instead.

"What's the haps?" I said.

He looked up, his eyes tired. "Same ole, same ole."

"Any news on the driver or the dead man or the truck or anything?"

"Interesting. They found a number on the interior of the trailer beneath a panel. Traced it to some drilling company in Oklahoma. Simpson, I think it was."

Bingo.

"Halleluiah, we hit pay dirt." I told him what I had pieced together about the Simpson drilling trucks, from Claymore's place to the Cimarron Breaks to the fields outside of Chisholm. I got really wound up and animated as I told him.

"Whoa. Pull in the reins, Jimmy. KBI came back with nada. Simpson Drilling had reported the trailer stolen two months ago. They're following up, but so far it's a no-go."

Damn. Another dead-end.

Still, something didn't seem right and I felt deep down inside there was some connection here that would fall into place, given time.

*****

Laura's red Vette sat in my drive and she sat on my porch steps.

"'bout time, O'Reilly. We got places to go, people to see and things to do."

"Maybe you do," I said. "But I got research to do and jobs to take care of. You know, it's the, I have to make a living and pay the rent kind of thing."

"Akira tells me you two have encountered some flak, and he has to take you on a journey."

"A journey? How does a mountain man who doesn't live in the mountains get around that much and communicate so well without any visible means of support? And he's not taking me anywhere." I said. "We spent half a day 'sanning' each other back and forth, and all we wound up with for our trouble was a missing mystery son named Toshi."

"I'm on my way to see Inez Gonzalez, Little Julio and Elena. I still think the children may hold some clue or information that can lead us to their mother and the other women. I really wish you would come with me."

"Look, Laura. This is difficult to say to you, but think about it. Think about how much time has elapsed. Those women are most likely long gone. Human traffickers aren't going to sit on their merchandise-"

"Merchandise?"

"I'm sorry. That's a cold hard fact and you know it. Little Julio and Elena's mother is probably in Indonesia by now, and there is nothing you or I can do about it. It's a sad fact, but a true one."

She lowered her head in acceptance. "I know," she said softly. "But I just can't let go of it. I have to try and do something."

I put my hand on her shoulder. "I'm sorry, Laura. I truly am sorry."

She stood up and walked toward her Vette. "I'm going out to talk with Inez Gonzalez. Come with me or not, I'm still going."

I watched her drive off as I sat on my porch, wondering at the injustices of the world and those that tried to right them.

A few minutes later I sat at my computer getting precious little information for the effort I put in. I sat back in frustration and thought about Laura. It was unfair of me not to give her the support she needed, no matter how wrong I thought she was. I was unfair to hang her out to dry when she was so passionate about her beliefs and causes. I was unfair not to give her the support she always gave me, even when she knew I was wrong. And I was wrong a lot.

As I walked out my front door and locked it behind me, I heard the phone ring. I started to get my door key out and decided against it. Whoever it was would leave a message. I got in my truck and headed out on the country roads north toward the address I had for the Gonzalez place.

Little did I know, I would never make it there.

16

A red Corvette sat at an angle, nose down, off the shoulder of the two-lane. Its right wheels sunk low into the ditch. It looked as if it had been run off the road.

I pulled up behind it, got out and looked around. Empty fields, blue skies and silence. That's all there was.

"Laura," I shouted out. Not once, but many, many times. "Laura, are you there?" I knew better, but hoped against hope that maybe she'd seen something, pulled off quickly and went to investigate. "Laura."

All I heard was the down and up cadence of a Bob White's call. Empty and lonely, its whistle hung on the air and defaulted to silence. Then, all I heard was the breeze rifling the leaves on the Osage Orange trees in the nearby windbreak.

I looked around. Laura's car was there. But there was no Laura. She was gone.

I opened the driver's door and looked in. Her keys were in the ignition. Her cell phone lay on the passenger side floor along with her purse. I took all three of them and contemplated what to do next. It seemed useless to go on to the Gonzalez place. Yet that was about all I could think of to do. I checked her car and found nothing else, so I headed north on the blacktop county two lane road.

Then I remembered the time when she bought me a throwaway cell phone for a job and made me carry it. She'd

96

shown me how to operate it, although I was still terrified by them. I pulled over, picked up her cell phone and studied it. I gingerly pushed a button, guessed right and pulled up her call log.

There it was, on the screen. Her last call was to me. Not ten minutes ago. That was the call coming in that I didn't open the door for.

It took me less than half the time to get back to my bungalow than it took me to get to her car. Laura would have been proud of me. I burst through the door and hit the red blinking message light on the phone.

Laura's voice was loud and fast.

"Somebody's following me, O'Reilly. Have been since I left your place. They're coming up on me faster now. Looks to be a white four door. Older model. Two riders. Both male. It's got a front plate, so it's probably out of state, but it's muddied over. It's closing in. Why the hell don't you carry a cell phone, O'Reilly? It's... oh, shit..."

I heard the clunk of her Corvette going in the ditch. Then the phone went dead.

*****

I stood waiting next to Laura's Corvette when Alex drove up in his Crown Victoria.

"Thanks, Alex. I appreciate you coming."

"I had to turn booking a public intoxication over to Jack, but I came a runnin' as soon as you called."

The two of us put on latex gloves and went over her car thoroughly, although I pointed out I had already contaminated the scene. We searched the area for footprints and signs of a struggle, but came up empty on all accounts. I was telling Alex about Laura's phone call and her description of the car pursuing her, as a police tow truck arrived and then hauled her Vette back to Chisholm.

"So what do we do now?" I said.

"I'll put out a bulletin, both about Laura and the car she described. We'll dust the car for prints, but like you said, it's already been contaminated. We'll do our best, but you know, these kinds of things are hard to deal with. Especially with so little to go on."

After he drove off in his cruiser, I stood next to my truck feeling lost and alone. One minute she's there and the next she's gone. And I didn't have a clue as to what to do. I drove back home and sat in my reading chair, depressed.

Time passed. I faded in and out of wakefulness and awareness. I don't know how much time elapsed, but when my eyes popped open, I looked around and Tiresias sat in the open French doorway, sightless, but staring up at me with the terrace and herbs behind him.

I drifted off again. It was as if he and Akira were one, and both invited me into their world, a world apart from my own creation, a world of light and energy. I gave in and entered. I saw images of tire tracks and water wells and Laura buried under earth and gasping for breath.

A yellow light of vibrant energy pulsed at me. It was unmistakably Laura's energy, telling me to follow the tracks and find her.

When I woke, it was the middle of the night and I lay slumped in my reading chair, sweating profusely. Tiresias was gone and the French doors were closed. I stumbled into my bed and slept the rest of the night, dreamless, and yet with a yellow energy pulsing into me.

*****

Late that same afternoon, unknown to me, two men, one in a flannel shirt and jeans, took the metal top and rusted riggings off of a dry, defunct cistern behind an old, abandoned farmhouse and next to a fallow field and trees of thorn-dense Osage Orange and Honey Locust. They left it tilted and partially covering the cavern below. Then they hoisted a woman up and over the edge and let her half-conscious body drop to the bottom.

Laura fell into an abyss. An abyss of the cistern and an abyss of the mind. She descended into a black hole, a world of darkness and webs and dank odors, and in her dizzying disorientation, she twisted and turned as she fell, scratching and clawing for some kind of hold. When she hit bottom, she lay in a heap of blurred confusion of both body and mind.

She felt around and defined the walls of her prison, crawling the best she could, the small perimeter of its confines. She looked up and saw a dim, thin shaft of light coming through a small opening surrounding the cistern's pump handle above her.

She thought this might be her end. An empty crypt sealed against the world. Doomed to a slow and painful death. A tomb of dark isolation where no one would ever discover her. She lay on the dirt floor and sank into an unconscious state of resignation.

*****

In the morning, when I woke a second time, I knew what I needed to do.

17

No phone rang when I exited my front door this time, but Baxter leaned against his black Towne Car in front of my house, dressed out in his dark suit and wraparound sun glasses, arms folded, waiting for me.

"We've got to stop meeting like this," I said. "People are starting to talk."

As I reached to open my truck door, he stepped in and put his hand on it, preventing me. "We need to talk some more," he said.

"I'm in a hurry. It's more than a little important."

"It'll have to wait."

"Look, Baxter. I've played your little game long enough. Tilt. Game over."

He reached into his suit coat, presumably toward a shoulder holster, but I kneed him in the groin. As he went down, I said, "I hate to play dirty, but enough's enough. Go find someone else to pester."

I drove off with him still curled up on my driveway. If William was looking out his window, he got an eye-full.

When I got to where Laura's car had gone off into the ditch, I kept driving. I passed two east-west, hard-packed crossroads, each with multiple tire tracks that had been made by vehicles who'd turned off the blacktop and onto the dirt county roads. Most of the tracks were wide and heavy, like farm equipment and trucks would make.

When I reached a third intersection, there was only one set of tracks and they headed west, so a maintainer had probably been down the road sometime the day before. These had to have been recent. They were smaller, more like a midsize car would make. About two miles down the road they cut sharply into a drive obscured by overgrown hedges and trees. Curiously, they came back out and continued further on down the road.

I turned in and slowly drove the rutted driveway until I came to an old, clapboard farmhouse. I parked, got out and looked around.

The farmhouse had broken-out windows, a sagging front porch and a front door that had been busted in. I started to walk in, but couldn't get past the door jamb for all the caved in floorboards.

Outside, nothing moved and the silence was eerie. I walked around the side of the house past a storm cellar entrance. When I lifted one door, a mass of cobwebs and dust choked off the opening. No one had been through there in quite some time.

In back of the house an old cistern sat rusting in the morning sun. It was bordered by a stretch of weedy, overgrown field dotted with Osage Orange and Honey Locust trees.

If the two men who Laura described on the phone message had brought her here, they had evidently moved on to somewhere else. Hence, the exiting tire tracks I'd noticed, going in a different direction. I stood listening to the silence and then turned to go back to my truck and follow the exiting tire tracks.

That's when it hit me, at the corner of the house. Sometimes you don't have to hear something, you just feel its presence. In the absence of sound or smell or sight, a manifestation makes itself known. Maybe it was a combination of Tiresias and Akira and something else unknown. Maybe it was just me imagining things. But I knew some force presented itself to me.

And then, the yellow pulsating light of energy I had felt the night before came at me again. It was Laura's presence. I knew it but I could not define it.

I turned around, but no one was there. I walked back to the cistern.

"Who's there?" I called out. And still, there was silence.

"Is anybody there?" I called out again, and waited. Nothing. I headed back to my truck, but then I heard it. A blunt, muted sound, like a moan in a sepulcher.

"Just a breeze in the trees," I said to myself, except out loud. Then I heard it again.

"No," I said. "Somebody's there."

Quiet. Silence. Then, there it was again. It was a hollow cry as if from a tomb, like wind blowing through an empty house, except no breeze was even stirring.

I kept talking out loud, but to myself as if someone else was with me. "It's coming from the cistern." I walked over to it and put my ear close to the metal cover and heard a stifled sound. It came up from deep down in the cistern.

It took several tries with my arms wrapped around the metal cover, but eventually I pulled it off of the cistern. "Laura," I called out into the well. "Laura. Is that you?"

Below, in her own circumscribed world, Laura crawled on her hands and knees through spider webs, touching splintered fragments of wood pierced by rusted nails and a discarded doll's head with hair that felt as soft and real as her own. There was only near and far, light and dark, sweet and musty. But then, light flooded her tomb at a diagonal and she heard a voice. She heard her name come at her like a needle, like a compass in a vast, open terrain.

"Yes," she said, in a faint cry. "Yes."

I recognized her voice and heaved a sigh of relief. I brought back a rope from my truck and lowered it down to her.

"Can you wrap this around yourself?" I yelled below. "Under your shoulders. Then tie it off. I'll pull you up."

I could feel the slack being taken up, slowly. She was conscious and pulled at the rope.

I pulled back and felt the rope go taught, and when I kept pulling I felt her body weight as it lifted off the floor of the well, and then I felt the inert weightlessness as she dangled in the air when her body inched up the side of the casing. Little expulsions of air burst out from her lungs.

It was slow progress, but I knew I could eventually pull her up and over the top.

Then, suddenly, my legs went out from under me. I toppled over on my side and heard her body hit bottom in the well. When I rolled over and looked up, some hulking presence stood over me and then came at me full force.

He wore a flannel shirt and jeans and swung a board at me as he advanced. Same man, different place.

"You got a thing about two-by-fours?" I said, laying on my back. "What's the obsession? Your mamma hit you with one?"

As I said it, I pushed off the wellhead and rolled away just as the two-by-four came down at me. I heard it hit the ground, bounce up and twang sideways off the metal wellhead. Flannel-man had leaned into it and lost his balance. He stumbled forward and fell to both knees.

I was up and on him in an instant. I kicked the two-by-four away, and pulled him up by his flannel shirt, then gave him an upper-cut to the solar plexus. He went down hard, and I thought I could resume my Laura exhumation. Time was of the essence. But he surprised me and was back up and coming at me. We clinched, and I rabbit punched him. He broke and countered, and then my old Bruiser the

103

Cruiser mentality took over with a one-two to the mid-section and a upper-cut to the jaw. He fell to his knees and stayed there.

I picked up the rope, caught my breath and steadied myself. But when I turned toward the cistern, Flannel-man was already back on me with a vengeance. This guy made more appearances than Freddy Kreuger. We sparred hard and I went down. I knew Laura's only chance at surviving, and maybe mine as well, was if I took this guy out. I summoned up the strength and charged him.

He grabbed me, but my momentum pushed him toward the trees a few feet away. We headed for a Honey Locust tree, his back being pushed directly at its clusters of thorns up and down the trunk, but a few yards from it he gained purchase and swung me around so my back was in position to be spiked.

Honey Locust thorns are sharp, thick mahogany colored spines, and the ones I saw were a good eight inches long. A mere scratch or pin prick from one will fester for days and swell a knee or elbow up twice its size, and I was in position for a full assault from the back.

My back was only a couple of feet from them when I went down on one knee, came up hard under Flannel-man, regained the momentum and swung him around. I pushed off and he went back and into the thorn clusters.

I heard the soft squish of flesh as the spikes sunk in, deep and hard, and at the same time, his death scream filled the air. One long thorn had penetrated all the way through his chest and protruded out, probably puncturing his heart, with blood streaming down his front. I hope the guy is a vampire, I thought. Then I could be known as Jimmy the Vampire Slayer. His head was upright, the skull having been pinned to the tree as well.

I assumed he was dead, but didn't take the time to check. Either way, he wasn't going anywhere. My arms had no strength left in them, so I got Laura's cell phone from

my truck, called 911, and waited at the wellhead,
comforting Laura down below until they arrived.

18

Laura sat upright in her bed at the hospital they took her to in Wichita. She could take nourishment and talk briefly, but was weak from her ordeal and bandaged with multiple lacerations. I'd been with her for two days as she drifted in and out of sleep, coherent at times, incoherent at others.

During that time, I had given much thought to getting back to my skip trace business and getting out of the unproductive chase I'd been on. The children had been saved, the women had not. Sometimes you had to learn to accept what was achievable and what wasn't.

Now, while she slept, I flipped through an old issue of a People magazine that featured short, glitzy profiles on prominent newscasters, many who had been in our fair city recently, and I kept dreaming up more schemes to humiliate them, like my Henderson Looper escapade, should any of them be foolish enough to return to my territory. Ah, the courage we have in our imaginations.

But my mind kept returning to the wellhead scene. It had taken EMS and firefighters two hours to extract Laura safely from the well, and also to deal with the remains of Flannel-man.

During that time, I waited anxiously and also gave details to Alex and Jack when they arrived. They had no idea who the dead wielder of two-by-fours was, but after processing the scene, they returned to Chisholm to start a search and investigation.

I had been torn between following the ambulance in to the hospital and trying to see if I could determine where the exiting tire tracks led to. I did follow the tracks west until they ended at the next blacktop crossroad. There, I noticed they angled to turn south on it. That meant they could be headed to Wichita, or to any number of the small towns in the vicinity. Then, I drove to the hospital, arriving shortly after the ambulance.

So, there I sat, bored enough to read People magazine and invent silly capers to antagonize idiotic newscasters.

Laura stirred and opened her eyes.

"What are you still doing here, O'Reilly?" Her voice was thin and faint.

"Some friend of mine got herself stuck in an old well, and I'm such a devoted, kind, obedient, cheerful, thrifty, brave, clean and reverent enough of a friend to want to keep tabs on her."

"Scout's honor?"

I raised the three fingers of my right hand. "Scout's honor."

"Thanks." Then she thought for a few moments, I guess, recollecting the incident.

"The well. Oh yeah, the well."

"Mmmm. It's a deep subject," I said.

She smiled a weak smile. "You're incorrigible."

"I can't help myself."

"Well," she paused for comic effect. "You need to get up off your lazy Irish butt-"

"Irish-American," I reminded her. "Fifth generation."

"Up off your lazy Irish-American, fifth generation butt, and get back on this case. I'm no good to you for awhile, so you'd better get hopping."

"Funny you should mention that. I've been thinking that we've taken this thing about as far as we-"

"Don't go there, O'Reilly. Don't even think of going there."

I figured I was on the losing end of a short argument, but I started to object anyway by giving her my "accepting what is achievable and what isn't" argument. Before I could, she got serious on me.

"Thanks, O'Reilly."

"I should have come with you," I said. "When you asked me to."

"Maybe. I don't know if I would have gone with you."

"Sure you would have. My bad, as Janie would say."

Laura smiled. "I don't remember a whole lot. When my car hit the ditch, I was out of it. I remember looking up and I saw a man standing over me with a syringe in his hand. I remember being lost in a waste land that stretched forever, and yet, I was enclosed in a tiny, tiny space. I felt like I crawled forever, but I had nowhere to go. I had the feeling that this was the end. That it was all over. That was a hopeless, lonely feeling. I thought about giving up."

I tried to think of some words of consolation, but they didn't come to me.

"Then I thought of all the women we need to save and how they are in some kind of wasteland and tiny space, too. I fought. I kept fighting, for myself and for them. But it didn't do any good. I remember seeing a yellow light going up and away from me. A yellow light that I think went to them and it went to you, too."

"Sure," I said. "A yellow light. I saw it, too." I tried to think of an explanation for it all when I was rudely interrupted.

An RN came in to take her vitals and give her some meds. "You'll have to excuse us for a couple of minutes, Sir."

I stood up. "No problem. I have to get up off my lazy Irish-American, fifth generation butt, anyway."

She gave me strange look as I walked out the door, closing it behind me. I could hear Laura chuckling as I left.

*****

Alex had his feet up on his desk and his head back. He was either dozing or deep in thought. I'd take odds on the dozing.

"Excuse the intrusion. What's the latest poop?"

He coughed and sputtered as he bolted upright in his swivel desk chair, planting his feet on the floor.

"You ain't gonna believe this, Jimmy. That man what got stuck to death by them thorns. It's like he never even existed. No ID on him. No prints in the database. No dental records. No distinguishing marks. No nothing. He's a nobody from nowhere."

"That's impossible. There has to be some record of him somewhere."

"If there is, we haven't found it. By the way. How's Laura?"

"She's doing okay. It's just going to take some time." I didn't go into how I'd planned on stopping the chase and how she'd goaded me into continuing.

"This guy is a dead-end."

"So to speak," I said.

"But I got some other news for you. That Robert Townsend truck driver fellow."

"One with the key and the missing finger?"

"Yep. We found out what the key went to."

"What was it?"

"His finger."

109

"Say again."

"The key went to his finger. You won't believe this Jimmy, but some janitor at that truck stop where his rig was found smelled something funny comin' outta one of the trucker lockers. They opened it up and found a bloody severed finger in it along with some other weird things. We've been coordinating and sharing info back and forth with their locals, so we got the key to them and it fit the locker. That ties it to Townsend."

"Are you saying Townsend cut off his own finger, put it in a locker and pocketed the key?"

"No. It ain't that. We don't know exactly what it is, other than peculiar. But at least we know that much more than we did. Look. I'll show you the pictures they faxed us." He pulled out two photos from different angles showing a bloodied finger laying next to an orange pompom and a purple cord with bells.

"What the hell are those things?"

"Nobody knows. It's orange, but it looks like them marshmallowy Hostess Sno Ball thingies we used to eat when we was kids. The cord? Who knows."

"This is the damndest thing, Alex. But I saw four of those exact orange things, same color and all, and a cord just like that one, just the other day." I told him about Akira and his costume.

"Sounds like we need to talk with this Akira guy."

"Maybe, but it'll have to be after I check on a skip trace job for Bomber and get directions from Laura. For the life of me, I can't remember how to get to Akira's place.

*****

When I walked through my open front door, a strange female sat on my living room couch.

I expected to see Janie, since the door was open, but instead, a long-legged teenager in short-short cut-offs and a tight fitting tee sat slouching on the couch, barefoot and with her arms crossed. She had a pale powdered face with jet black dyed hair and black painted lips and a ring through the lower lip. She stared down at the floor.

"Hello," I said.

"Ugh," was all I got back from her, and she didn't look up at me.

I went out through my open French doors where Janie stood on the terrace watering my herbs from a sprinkler can. "Janie, there is a stranger sitting on my couch. I mean, a strange, stranger."

"Yeah. That's Zoey." She squinted at me.

I squinted back, unconsciously. "And she is..." I left it hanging.

"Oh, she's a friend of mine from school. I hope you don't mind I brought her along. She had a rough time at school today and I wanted to cheer her up."

"It doesn't look like it's working."

"Oh, she's a lot better than she was. She got into trouble because she dropped the F-bomb on a teacher in class."

"The F-bomb? I can see where that would get you into trouble. But you know, maybe she's not the best person for you to be hanging out with."

"She's okay. She's really sensitive, and she likes poetry, too, only a different kind from what you've shown me. She's reading this guy named Lawrence Ferlinghetti and it's something about your mind and Coney Island. Really weird, and it has some bad language in it. But it's cool."

"Ferlinghetti will certainly broaden your perspective on poetry," I said. "I guess you could do worse."

She finished watering and walked back inside. "I got something to show you, Mr. O." I followed and she handed me a sheet of paper off my reading table. "Look. W.B. wrote you a poem."

"Your puppy wrote a poem for me?"

I guess my voice gave away my incredulousness, because she blushed and quickly said, "Well, I really wrote it, but it's like him talking. So, it's like he wrote it. See, he autographed it for you."

At the bottom there was a dried muddy paw print. I read the poem and said, "This is great, Janie. You should... I mean, W.B. should keep writing. He's got some talent."

She smiled a big, wide smile, and then said, "Gotta go. Come on, Zoey."

I wasn't sure Zoey had enough life in her to actually move, but she dutifully stood and towered a full head over and above Janie, and that was still with the slouch. She still hadn't said anything coherent, but she finally looked at me, made eye contact and grunted one word. "Cool."

"Yeah. Cool." I was beginning to sound like a teenager and I didn't particularly like it. "Wait a minute, Janie. Let me give you something." I walked over to my book shelf, pulled a thin volume of poems by Don Marquis, and handed it to her.

"This is entitled *Archy and Mehitabel*. Archy is a cockroach and his best friend is Mehitabel the cat. Since Archy is a cockroach, he can't hit the shift key on a typewriter at the same time he jumps on the other keys, so all his poems are in lower case letters with no capitalization."

"What's a typewriter?" said Zoey.

"It's like an old-time word processor," said Janie. "You know. Before computers."

"You mean we haven't always had computers?"

Janie looked at me and shrugged her shoulders. "Thanks. Wow. A cockroach that writes poetry. W.B. is really going to like this. I'll read it to him tonight."

"Let me know what he thinks of it," I said.

They were out the door, Janie bouncing in the lead and Zoey shuffling behind. I stood shaking my head in disbelief. Teenagers.

19

A light rain fell as I jogged my way around a morning section run. One mile west. North another one mile. East. South and then west back home. Low gray clouds socked the entire area in and the coolness of the rain on my face and the soaked tee-shirt felt good.

It hadn't been forecast, so the surprise of it caught me off guard, but perhaps its coming portended an end to the long parched season we'd had. The farmers would welcome it. That was certain.

It felt more than good. It felt cleansing, as if the moisture coursing down my face and arms was washing more than the dust away. It flushed out all the darkness and decay I had been surrounded by recently.

Perhaps that is what Akira had been after by standing naked under his man-made waterfall. Purification. That's what Laura had referred to it as and that's what it seemed like to me. I felt purified.

*****

"Glad to see you're still on it, O'Reilly."

I stood at the foot of Laura's hospital bed listening to her go on and on about how I was a quitter and a whiney little boy and if it wasn't for her, blah, blah, blah.

"Yeah, yeah. I just dropped in for some information. You think you could cut the verbal abuse long enough to answer a couple of questions? We have a lead and I need to ask Akira something. Could you give me directions to his place by the Cimarron Breaks?"

"I can do better than that. They're turning me lose. Doing the paperwork as we speak. Wait an hour and I'll go with you."

"Nope. They may be letting you out of here, but you're going home and you know it. You still have a lot of recuperating to do. Besides, I've got a skip trace job to take care of first."

She hung her head as she realized the truth of the recuperation point, and then gave me directions.

"Thanks. I'm also hoping to meet his wife when I go this time, if she's there."

"His wife?" She looked puzzled. "His wife is dead."

"Dead? What are you talking about? No. He told me his wife came here with him to help get their son back."

"O'Reilly, his wife is deceased. She died in the Kobe earthquake in ninety-five."

I wasn't in a mood to argue, and then I realized I might not even need the directions she'd given me. "You know those fluffy pom-pom things hanging on Akira's costume? And that purple bungee cord thing with bells that he had?"

"It's called a *suzukake*."

"The pom-poms are called sue-sue-cake?"

"No. The traditional garment is. It's not a costume. And it's pronounced sue-zu-ka-kay, which is a jacket, and *hakama*. Leggings. Traditional clothing."

"Excuse me for confusing them. Do you know what the pom-poms or bungee cord with bells is for?"

"No. I do not." She was emphatic. "But the least you could do is show some respect for the tradition, even if you don't understand it."

End of conversation.

"Glad you're feeling better," I said, as I walked out the door.

*****

I waited for one, Gregory Simpkins, AKA The Gopher, outside of a bar in the Delano District on West Douglas in Wichita. Gopher, his street name, was in part due to his looks. He had an overbite and a slanted jaw, along with small beady eyes and little ears that looked like they were pinned back. The only thing he lacked was the fur. But the moniker was also due to the fact that he used to be a low-level hack who ran numbers for racketeers before the State legalized the lottery.

I didn't have to wait long. Simpkins stepped out of the front door of the bar and stopped. He shielded his eyes as they adjusted from the dark bar to the daylight, and I stood next to him before he could see me.

"Gregory." I couldn't bring myself to call him Gopher.

He staggered away a couple of steps, both from surprise and from a few too many beers, I supposed.

"It's me, Gregory. Jimmy O'Reilly." We had done business, so to speak, a number of times before. "Bomber needs to see you about your last bail post."

"I- I can't right now, Mr. O'Reilly. I gotta-"

I patted the small bulge under my shirt. His eyes had adjusted and he stared at the hidden Ruger and acquiesced. I helped him in my truck and had him in front of Bomber on South Seneca within ten minutes. Easy job. This time. You just never know.

When I exited Bomber's I turned to go to a diner at the other end of the strip mall. It was already mid-afternoon and I was starving, but then I thought if I waited much longer, the trip to the Cimarron Breaks and back would get me in long after dark. I made an immediate about-face to head back toward my truck, and ran smack into someone standing there. Literally, ran into him. I jumped back and caught my breath.

"You again. Akira, you've got to stop doing this to me."

"Jimmy-san, you-"

"Hold it right there. Let's don't start sanning each other. We'll be here the whole afternoon. How did you get here anyway?"

"No matter."

He stood there in his jeans and tee-shirt, with his Aikido stick slung over his back. "You always carry that with you?" I said. He simply nodded yes. "Look, I was on my way to see you. I've got some questions, so if we can find a place to talk it'll save me the trip down there."

"Good. Come and we will have something to eat while we talk."

That didn't take any convincing. He had me drive to a brick-paved back street in an old rundown business area, and we walked into an establishment that looked like it had been cobbled together in a narrow space between two deteriorating buildings. There were no windows and it had no sign on the outside except for a small red cloth with two white kanji on it, hung over the door. The place looked as if it was uninhabited. At least, until we got inside.

Inside, it was a different world. There were low-slung tables around the room, most of them occupied, with paper half-partitions between them for privacy. Each table had tatami mats on the floor to sit on. Shamisen, or a three stringed banjo as Akira explained, twanged in the background as if Kabuki actors were going to jump out at us. The dimly lit space was filled with a mingling mixture of competing aromas, and even if I wasn't starving, the smells would have driven me crazy.

Akira sat effortlessly. I looked around for a chair. There were none, so I struggled placing my legs and feet and finally just sat against the wall for back support and stretched my legs straight out under the low table. A woman in a traditional kimono and obi sash said something to Akira and he answered in Japanese.

"I hope you like sashima," said Akira.

"Actually, I was hoping for some ravioli in a brown-butter and sage sauce with a glass of red."

He called the woman back, said something else to her and then said to me, "I think you will be pleased. Rather curious though. An Irish-American man who prefers Italian food."

"No more curious that you. A Japanese man who can pronounce his Ls. Now that's curious."

"Ah yes. Engrish vely good. Yes? You rike way I speak Engrish?"

"Okay, Akira. You got me on that one. What I wanted to ask you-"

"Not now. We will eat first and then ask questions later."

"That's better that shoot first and ask questions later." I smiled.

He smiled back and said, "I get it. One of your famous sayings? Yes?"

The woman returned, setting down a blue and white ceramic beaker with two small cups. She gave me chopsticks along with a fork, thankfully, and chopsticks to Akira. Then she placed a plate of raw fish and a plate of steaming pasta in front of both of us, obviously meant to be shared. There were also two bowls of dipping sauces next to the pasta.

"Ravioli?" I said.

"No. Gyoza. Pot stickers, you call them." He poured from the beaker into the cups. "First, we toast." We each lifted our cup, and he said, "*Kampai*. One of our sayings. It means, drain the cup."

"Sayings? Oh, like when you said you had no face to show? Well then, *kampai*," I said, and added 'Cheers.' And when I downed it, a warm, silky glow spread down my throat and into my torso.

"I couldn't get you red wine, so hot sake will have to do." He immediately poured two more.

"It'll do." I tried the chopsticks, but the pot stickers kept sliding off. I had absolutely no skill with them at all. On one try, my chopsticks awkwardly touched his in the bowl, and Akira got very animated.

"No. Never do that. A very bad thing to do in our culture."

I assumed it was a matter of hygiene, apologized, and picked up my fork to use. When I bit into the pot stickers, they tasted of rich garlic along with sesame oil and ginger. Dipped in the hot chili sauce, all the flavors burst out at once on my palate. I had never tasted anything like it. "What a delicacy," I said.

He smiled. "Pan-fried on one side and steamed on the other."

"All right, Akira," I said when we finished. "The next time we dine, it's at my place and I'll fix you hand-made ravioli with a glass of Italian red. Then you'll compare. Deal?"

"Deal. Now we will ask questions. *Kampai*." We drained the cups, the last of the saki, and he ordered another beaker-full. The warmth had now spread into my limbs as well.

"Before I ask about the Yakuza, I have to ask a personal question. When we sat on the hill by the river, you said your wife was there with you."

"She was."

"But Laura said she is deceased."

"She is."

"I'm confused. How can your wife be with you and be dead? Either she's alive or she isn't."

"Do not think, either-or. Think, both-and."

"Isn't that a little contradictory?"

"Yes and no."

"Now I'm really confused."

"She is here now."

I looked around. "The waitress? Is that your wife? She's alive?"

"No. My wife is dead, but her *ki* is with us, now, as we speak. *Ki*. Her energy. Her spirit. She is with me always, helping me, guiding me. Jimmy-san, your wife is deceased also. Yes? We will talk about this again, another time, and how do you say it? Compare writing. You see, I can pronounce my 'Ls' but I do not understand your idioms. Your sayings."

"Compare notes is the saying," I said. "I learned a Japanese saying and now you've learned a new English one. Okay, here is my next question." I was starting to feel a little woozy from the sake, so I had to concentrate hard. "What are those orangey things on your costume? I mean, your *suzukake*? And that cord you carried with the bells on it? And what significance do they have?"

"Ah, my *suzukake*. Someone has taught you a Japanese word. First, the six pom-poms, as you call them, symbolize the six virtues. If I encountered another Yamabushi in the Cimarron Breaks," he covered his mouth and giggled at that absurdity, "we would recognize each other from a brotherhood. Then, the cord with bells represents safety in times of dangerous passages. It is an umbilical cord to take us over deep chasms of danger. Now, why do you ask?"

"Because both of these items were found along with a severed finger."

He looked off and drew a long, deep breath, and then let it out. "This is not good."

"I didn't figure it was. But I thought maybe you could shed some light on the subject."

"Shed light? An idiom I do not understand."

"Explain. Can you explain it all?"

He thought for a moment, and then explained the significance of the severed finger. "Whenever the Yakuza wants to discipline someone, or make a statement so all will recognize who is in charge, they take a portion of the little finger for emphasis. So no one will misunderstand, including, of course, the victim."

"What about the pom-poms and chord?"

"That is a problem to understand. I think they are telling someone that they will need all their virtue and all the safety available to them if they are to survive. And they seem to assume this person will understand the meanings. Me, perhaps? It is a cautionary message."

"These were left in a trucker's locker in Oklahoma. I don't see how they could have been meant for you. Also, the man that belonged to the severed finger is dead."

"As I said. This is not good."

I leaned back against the wall and thought for a long minute. "I'm not sure where to go next."

"We go get some rest."

He took me literally. "I mean-"

"I know what you mean. That idiom I understand. But look at the time and look at how much we have had to drink."

He was right. It was early evening and I was much more than a little woozy now. In fact, I'd had way too much sake to drive.

We walked, sort of, staggered is more like it, a few blocks to an old brownstone near East High. Akira sang some Japanese song, loudly, as we weaved our way along the sidewalk. There is a one room walkup in the rear of the complex that Bomber could never rent, at least to anyone he could trust, so he gave me the key for whenever I was working a skip trace and needed to stay in the city.

That's where Akira learned another English idiom: Crashed for the night.

20

The needle on my gas tank pointed to empty. I'd spent the entire morning driving the area where I'd seen the tire tracks of the car involved in Laura's kidnapping and had nothing to show for it.

When we woke in the morning, Akira insisted, against my protests, that I follow my one lead and that he go his own way in search of his son Toshi, which he felt would take him to the Yakuza. Eventually, he said, we would meet up.

I knew this was a futile errand and I was mad I let him talk me into it. In fact, it was so boring, my mind had wandered and I didn't really concentrate on the task at hand.

Instead, I mused about my ancestors and the violence that has followed me all my life. It didn't just begin with those immigrant O'Reillys in Runnymede. It went back much, much farther. Back in the thirteenth century, O'Reillys were the Lords of East Breifne, Ireland. What is now County Cavan. We carried long-handled axes, swords and pikes, fighting on horseback and foot, slashing, clubbing, spiking and hacking our enemies. We served under the O'Neills in a futile attempt to repulse the English invaders, and took a thorough beating for our efforts.

We had always been a tough, determined and violent family, as well as astute financiers. We even minted our own coins, known as the Reilly. The money aspect never stuck with me, but the violence would be with me forever. I just couldn't seem to shake it.

I came out of my reverie long enough to realize I needed gas and I needed it quickly. Fortunately, I was on the edge of a small town with one gas station. I turned off the two-lane and drove down the main street toward it.

That's when it passed me going the other way. The car Laura had described on the phone message. An older, white four door car with front pates that were muddied over. I hit my brakes to turn around, and then realized I could go nowhere if I didn't get gas. The station was in the next block, so I pulled in, keeping an eye on which way the white car turned.

I filled only about a third of the way up to save time, jumped back in and took off. Back on the two-lane, the white car was nowhere to be seen. I floored it and within two minutes I had it in my sights, so I slowed down and kept a respectable distance.

He drove in the general direction of Wichita, but veered off as he approached an area on the outskirts where several industrial plants stood. When he got to a meat processing plant, a large complex of buildings, he turned in and parked in their massive parking lot. I put my truck in a slot well away, but where I could observe him as he got out and walked to a gated entrance with a sign that read: Employees Only. Personnel Division.

While I waited, I thought over the situation. If this guy had been working with Flannel-man, the connections were becoming more evident to me. When he tried to scare me off, Flannel-man said he represented individuals who employed him to see that their interests were protected. He also said that industry around here depended on employment that required certain kinds of individuals.

If two plus two equals four, the sum of it all seemed pretty apparent to me. These guys were at least one link in the chain of getting illegals here to work for some of the local industry. A meat packing plant was certainly an obvious end-point for that kind of scheme. The question was, where in the chain did their link fit? Flannel-man claimed no knowledge of Baxter or Claymore. Maybe that was true. Maybe it wasn't. Were they connected to the Yakuza?

I got out, walked over to his car and bent down to look at the mud covered plates. Up close, I could see the designation at the top. It read Chihuahua. A state in Mexico, just across the border. Curious, because neither of these guys looked Hispanic.

I considered trying the door to see if it was unlocked, when I spotted him coming out the gate. I got back in my truck and followed him out the lot and back toward the town he came out of. Except this time he drove on past the town on the two-lane, going farther north, past field corn and combines.

He turned off on a hard-packed county road. It had a small sign off and away from the corner, barely visible, that read Wholesale Nursery, with an arrow pointing to the west. As I oriented myself, I realized we were not too far from the place with the well where they'd taken Laura.

About a mile down the road, just over a rise that hid what was beyond it, we came to a nursery operation that appeared gigantic. It stretched out as far as the eye could see, with trees and bushes of all sizes lined up in balls of soil. The place was fenced, with concertina wire across the top, held in place by metal Y-joints. Whoever ran this place didn't want visitors and went to great lengths to keep unwanted people out.

I stopped at the gate where the white car entered. A large sign said: NURSERY. WHOLESALE ONLY. A gigantic, hulking man stood guard outside of a little hut with a pointed top, like you'd see at a border crossing in an old World War Two movie.

I pulled up to the gate. He opened it and let me in. I couldn't believe my luck, as I saw the white car in the distance drive toward a metal fabricated structure and park. I felt I was on the verge of cracking this thing wide open. I rolled down my window and looked up at the gatekeeper.

"Just looking for some landscaping options for a client," I said. "Where can I find the Pin Oaks?"

"To your right. Row MM. Turn left and go about a quarter of a mile." He was tall and muscular and looked menacing. Like a bouncer in a bar.

"Thanks." I started to roll my widow up.

He stuck a wooden object that looked suspiciously like a billy club in my window and prevented it from closing. "Just a minute, Pal. I need to see your number."

"My number?"

"Your wholesaler's ID number."

"718429." Ingeniously, I made it up. Clever of me, but it didn't quite work.

"That doesn't compute. Let me see your card."

"Sorry", I said. "My turtle ate it."

He looked at me strangely, and then shoved the club in on my forehead, pushing my head back against the headrest on my seat.

"We don't take kindly to gatecrashers. You'd best back on out of here and go your own way, Pal."

Damn. I'd almost made it. "I'll re-up my wholesaler's membership and be back next week," I said. "My client won't be happy. I promised him some Pin Oaks for tomorrow."

He watched as I backed out and headed further west on the county road. A little ways down, I parked on the other side opposite the sprawling nursery compound, behind a hedgerow. I could see the gated entrance from there, and the keeper of the gate couldn't see me. For all he knew, I was long gone.

About a half hour later, the white car emerged from the gate, so I fired up my truck and headed back to follow it. When I passed the gate, the billy club toting gatekeeper watched me go on by. I saw him in my rearview as he took out a cell phone and punch in some numbers.

I should have been a little more astute about what was going on, but I was too single-minded of purpose about trailing the white car with Chihuahua plates to notice. In fact, I saw him ahead of me lift a cell phone to his ear almost immediately after the billy club man hoisted his own. Hello. Can you put one and two together?

I crested the rise I'd gone over earlier, on my way there, and there he was, the white car crosswise, blocking the road. And him leaning against the door.

I pulled up short, got out and faced him. "You're in a shit-load of trouble, Buddy. I got a friend who spent an afternoon at the bottom of a well, and she still isn't feeling too well." The sound of two wells in one sentence didn't ring true, and when I looked over my shoulder to see what he was staring at, I knew why. A giant quad-cab truck with monster elevated wheels crunched down on the hardpan behind me. The billy club man, along with another hulk, descended from the truck and advanced on me.

"I'd say you're the one in a shit-load of trouble," said the man from the white car.

I looked both ways, then in my truck at my baseball bat I carry and the cutaway where my Ruger was hidden, but realized it was too little too late. I looked out at the open field to the south, my only option for escape.

"You'd best come with us. Nowhere to run, Pal." This was the billy club man. "Bubba, you bring his truck back."

I looked at the other hulk. "Bubba? Is that your real name?"

He didn't bother to answer. "If it is," I said, "I know some pig farmers in the next section over who'd like to meet you."

Still no answer. "They know how to play a banjo real good."

Warped humor didn't seem to be getting me anywhere, because the next thing I knew, I had one hulk on each side of me, and they unceremoniously tossed me in the back seat of the quad-cab. I began to think the driver of the white car was right. 'twas I who was in a shit-load of trouble.

The last thing I remember was being tied to a chair, á la Flannel-man mode. Except this time there was no two-by-four.

Instead, someone came toward me holding a hypodermic needle.

21

Akira Sato sat seiza style on a high sloped bank of the Arkansas River which looked out at the Keeper of the Plains statue near the sacred confluence in the distance. It was a strange mix of cultures, and yet he felt at ease meditating there. He took in strong universal energy that calmed his mind and his spirit and gave him direction. He knew that his new-found friend was in trouble.

His eyes were closed, yet suddenly he felt the presence of another. In fact, a thin Asian man in sunglasses, and with full body tattoos which were hidden beneath his sharkskin suit stood behind him. The man stepped around him and laid a small box on the ground in front of him. He bowed, ever so slightly, and then disappeared.

Akira opened his eyes and looked down at the box. He didn't need to open it, as he knew what it contained. Yet, irresistibly drawn, he gently picked it up, took the lid off of it and set it at the base of his knees.

He looked down at Toshi's natal ring he always wore on his little finger. Nestled next to it was the severed first joint of the little finger.

*****

"Damn him." Laura sat in her condo, listening to Jimmy O'Reilly's recorded message on his answering machine. When it beeped to leave a message, she said "Get yourself a cell phone, O'Reilly. I'm tired of this." And then hung up.

She nibbled on delivered pizza and sipped a Cosmopolitan from a martini glass, bored and trying to think of what to do next. She drained the Cosmo and started to mix another in the cocktail shaker, when the doorbell rang.

"Akira, what are you doing here?"

He stood in her open doorway staring intently at her. "Jimmy-san needs our help. We must go to him."

"Great. The only problem is finding him."

Just then, her phone rang.

22

I woke up to a body that felt like someone had taken a ball peen hammer to every muscle and joint in it, and also, I awoke to total darkness. I had no idea what they had put into my body with the syringe, but at least it hadn't killed me. But I had no idea where I was.

As much as I hurt, I also felt suspended, as if I was floating, and yet at the same time there was a tremendous pressure on my chest and legs. I felt a metal object on one wrist, and it seemed as if it was attached to some kind of rod or structure. With my free hand I could feel what seemed like sand, as if I was stuck in a giant pile of it. I wondered if I was still under the influence of whatever they gave me, and hallucinating myself into the setting of some Kafka story or maybe a Dali painting.

When my eyes adjusted, I made out the semblance of a metal wall, like the interior of a shed, except now I saw that it was curved and rose up high above me. I was handcuffed, shackled to a metal ladder which went up the side of the structure, and my body sunk into sand up to my chest, except it wasn't sand. It was grain. Harvested corn kernels.

Then the reality of it began to set in. They, or someone, had put me in a grain silo. I was cuffed to a ladder in a grain silo with corn that came maybe half way up and I was stuck up to my chest in it. I tried to rise up in the grain, but the pressure was too great, and what little movement I could make seemed to suck me down farther, almost like quicksand.

I quit moving and tried to control my panic so I could breathe. I felt as if I was suffocating, so I took measured breaths and found my chest could indeed rise and fall and take in air under the grain's pressure, and then I began calculating my chances.

If this was some farmer's silo out in the middle of a field, it might be days before anyone would come out to it, and no one would likely hear my screams. I might not even be found until the middle of winter when the silage was being used for livestock feed. But no, that's not what this was. The structure was too large for a farm silo. This was a commercial storage silo. With the field corn harvest in full swing, workers would be here and about, and on a daily basis. I had every hope in the world, now, that I would be found.

But then the terrible truth of my circumstances sank in and hit me full-force. No one would ever hear me. No one would ever find me until months later when the grain was being loaded and shipped off on railcars for feed processing.

Once the grain trucks started rolling in with today's loads from the fields, once the machinery was set in motion and the conveyor belts began moving, once gears and metal were grinding, no one would hear any kind of sound I could make inside the silo. The machine noise would be too deafening. It would drown out whatever human sounds were around.

One of two ends was certain for me. When the corn came tumbling in, down through the small opening at the silo's top, either my lungs would fill with grain dust and I'd choke to death, or I'd be buried under tons more of the grain and suffocate. Either way, my fate was sealed.

It's strange what you think about in moments like these, when you're certain you are close to breathing your last and there is no possible means of escape, when there is no available avenue or exit, and hope simply is not a word that exists for you.

I thought of saffron threads. Tiny orange-yellow threads. Their pungent smell. I thought of how, in some far, remote corner of the world, it took someone's hand to pick three threads from each purple crocus flower, until thirteen thousand of them combined to make one ounce, so I could order them from a catalogue at some exorbitant price and store them in my pantry, and then use them to color and flavor a risotto or a pilaf or a bouillabaisse.

What kind of a touch, what kind of a gentle touch did it take from a human hand on a frail flower petal to do such delicate work? Did those stained fingers go home and touch a child's cheek or hold a husband's hand, or cook a meal of their own? Who was I by virtue of my money to claim their precious possessions?

Then, all of a sudden, I heard gears mesh. Metal hit metal. And the wanderings of my mind stopped abruptly as machine noise ratcheted up. I had enough play in the cuff chain that I began banging it against the side of the silo, more metal-on-metal, even though I realized it was a useless exercise in futility.

I started yelling and screaming at the top of my lungs, and all the while kept banging the metal-on-metal of handcuffs against the side of the silo. I felt my body slide ever-so-slowly farther down into the quicksand of grain that engulfed me. I was up to my arm pits now, and dry kernels of corn rose up and caked around my lips. I spit out corn as fast as I could and kept shouting. Grain began tumbling from far above and splattering all around me, rising up even farther on my face. I tilted my head back so I could keep sucking in air. Pure panic was setting in.

Then, machinery grinded to a halt. Silence. I heard somebody shout, "We're losing it. It's not open all the way, it's spilling down the outside."

There was a clatter of footsteps on top of the silo and I heard metal creak as somebody manually pulled back the opening above. I kept flailing my one cuffed arm against the metal wall and yelling the best I could, but grain started sifting into my mouth and my tongue went dry. I tilted my head back even farther, as far as it would go so I could keep air coming in. But grain started to fall into my throat and to choke me.

Then I heard whoever was up-top. "Hey, somebody's down in there. I can hear somebody yelling. Who's there?"

Ten minutes later a worker stood above me on the ladder and used bolt cutters to snap off the cuffs. Then, a rope was lowered, put under my arms, and I heard the joyful sound of machinery lift me up and out of my quagmire of seeds, and I spit kernels out my mouth as I rose.

On the ground outside the silo in brilliant sunlight, coop workers and grain truck drivers stared in disbelief, and an ambulance pulled into the complex. I was still dazed, sitting there in the blazing sun and gasping for breath.

But even then, out of the corner of one eye, I thought I saw one of the hulks. He'd seen me pulled up and out of my tomb of grain, and knowing I had not been buried alive like they'd planned, he strode to the quad-cab, backed out and sped away from the scene.

I had to find a way to gather my senses, get oriented and tell somebody, anybody, about the meat processing plant and the white car and the two hulks and the quad-cab and the hypodermic needle and the nursery.

23

"**There was this meat processing plant** and a white car and there were two hulks with a quad-cab, and they had a needle and a nursery."

Alex stood next to a uniformed man he called Bob, the Halstead Chief of Police. They were at the foot of my bed in the Halstead hospital. Alex rolled his eyes a little half roll after my statement. I had just woken from whatever the paramedics gave me to calm me down and I knew I was making no sense, yet that was all I could say.

"Jimmy," Alex said. "I come up here when Bob here called me about what all happened. But I gotta say, you ain't making a whole lot of sense. We need to hear what happened exactly. Can you just sorta start at the beginning and go easy?"

I rationally tried to explain all that happened, and when I finished, I don't know if it all made sense or not. But about that time, Laura and Akira knocked on my door and then joined us.

"I gave Laura a call," said Alex. "Let her know where you were. Hope you don't mind."

Laura and Akira smiled at me. Akira put out a hand and touched my foot, and I felt a lightning charge of white light and energy shoot up my leg, arc over my head and pulse down my other side. It calmed me and gave me a clarity of mind.

"Reiki?" I said.

He just smiled.

Bob stepped forward and looked down at me. "We need to be clear on exactly what transpired. More specifically, we need to know precisely where these nurserymen are you claim abducted you, and where their nursery is located."

He left after I explained it all, and then Alex said, "I'll be in touch, but you need to pull in the reigns, Boy. You're a little too anxious outta the stall, trying to do things you shouldn't be a trying to do."

"I know this is all related," I said. "What just happened to me and what happened to Laura, the importation of illegals, the severed finger and the Yakuza, and Lon Claymore, too. They all have to be connected somehow."

"You got any grand conspiracy theories? Trilateral Commission or deep space aliens or any such a thing?"

I shook my head. "No. Just hunches."

*****

My bungalow was like Grand Central Station. People came and went constantly. How was a recuperating guy supposed to get some rest?

After they discharged me from Halstead Hospital, with the admonition to stay at home alone and rest until fully recovered, I did exactly as I was told. Except for the alone part. Akira stayed with me to keep an eye on me, Laura stopped in to check on me, Alex came by with updates and Janie was in and out with all of her chores and friends. And that was only the half of it. Way too much excitement for a convalescing skip tracer.

We set up a makeshift tatami mat on the floor for Akira to sleep on, and the first night I fulfilled my promise to Akira, fixing him and Laura handmade ravioli.

I mixed my dough with durum semolina flour and eggs, using the countertop well method, and then rolled the sheets out on my hand crank pasta maker. Starting at the widest setting, I narrowed it down to the thickness for ravioli, and then spaced the filling on the dough. My filling consisted of Tuscan white beans, caramelized onion, spinach, celery and garlic. When I put the top sheet of dough on, I used my crimp-cutter to seal and cut the pasta pillows, and then cooked them just to al dente.

The very process itself helped to give me clarity of mind, calm my soul and return me to a rational state of being.

I served my Tuscan bean ravioli in a brown-butter sauce with sautéed shallots and chopped sage from my terrace garden. This was accompanied with a simple Caprese salad. For it, I managed to get fresh buffalo mozzarella and some heirloom tomatoes, so along with basil from my terrace and my best imported olive oil, it was as big a hit as the ravioli.

Of course, only a Brunello would suffice as the wine of choice.

"How does that compare with your pot stickers?" I said.

"Sorry. No comparison." Akira looked at me seriously, and then smiled. "Two pastas and so different you can't compare them. Both wonderful. Just like you can't compare the Brunerelli, or whatever you call that wine, with the sake.

After Laura left, Akira and I finished off what remained of the Brunello while we sat in my reading area having a lively conversation about death. We shared stories about our wives and how we had tried to find ways to cope with their violent ends.

I told him of Sondra's murder in a convenience store holdup several years earlier, and he told me of the devastation after the Kobe earthquake and finding out how his wife, Miko, perished in it.

"The other day, you said your wife is always with you. Her spirit, or *ki* as you called it, is always with you, guiding you."

"Yes."

"I didn't understand then, but after thinking about it, it makes sense. I'd never thought about it that way, but Sondra has been with me, too. She comes to me in dreams and even brings me comfort in little ways only she could. In one dream, she told me to find an abiding peace. And since then, I believe I have. I see it all around me in something as small as a brittle oak leaf turned orange-red in the fall, or in the flapping of a heron's wings as it takes off from the river."

"Yes. Why do you think I live in the Cimarron Breaks? There is a beauty there. I think your word is stark. A stark beauty. What you called an abiding peace. Now you must let go. It doesn't mean she won't still be with you. Only that you must release her and release yourself, as well."

"But, I don't know how. I don't know how to get there."

"Yes, you do. It is what we call the Gateless Gate."

"How can a gate be gateless?"

"You are in a place where it looks like you have to pass through a gate to get somewhere you need to be. But when you do, you look back and see that there was no gate there in the first place. A Gateless Gate. It means you are already there. Even though you are here, you are already there. You just don't see it."

"That's impossible."

"No, it is not. Another old saying is that it is like Selling Water by the River. There is no need for water if the river is there. But we go on selling it and you go on buying it anyway, because you do not see the river."

"I'm more confused than ever. I don't get it."

"You will. Let me tell you a story about Miko's death. It begins with my childhood."

"You knew your wife as a child?"

"No. That comes later. As a child, a Sanka woman came to our door one day. Sanka are the Japanese version of what you call Gypsies. She spent the day weaving baskets for us, and I was captivated by her beauty. After she left, I took one of my mother's small wooden eggs and carved the woman's face on it. I never even knew I had the ability to do something like that.

"Everyone was so astounded, I just kept on carving. Image after image. I even made my own wooden eggs. Then one day, some men came and gave me money to carve eggs, and they kept coming back with more money for more carved eggs. I was so happy with my artistic talent, I never sought the reason for their purchases. It wasn't until I was much older that I found out the real reason.

"The men were Yakuza, and the different shades of wooden eggs and designs were sent to those who were being punished, as a message. One style of egg meant you were going to lose a finger. Another meant death. I could not accept this messenger of death that I was a part of. When I left our region, I thought I left the evil behind.

"But many years later, when I came down from the mountains into the city after the earthquake, into the rubble and devastation where over six thousand lost their lives, hoping to find my wife alive, I was given much help and support. But not from who you would think. The Yakuza came and gave millions in money and food and shelter to the victims. But they also personally helped me to discover Miko's fate and gave me comfort when I did."

"The same Yakuza that cuts off fingers and deals in human flesh?"

"Yes. The same. There is a duality in their being. Yet there is no duality. They are one and the same. They are what they are. So you see, I have had violence follow me, just as you have had violence follow you. I must come to terms with that, just as you must come to terms with your duality and sameness."

"It still doesn't make sense."

"For me, I know that my son, Toshi, who was ten years old when his mother died, saw all that happened and took it in. Perhaps that is what drew him to become part of the Yakuza here. Now, I must accept the past and know that what is here and now is evil. No matter the past, I must act on what is happening now."

"Then we are agreed," I said. "We have to go in search of your son as well as answers."

"Yes. We do."

"Tomorrow, we'll devise a plan and figure out what to do. A course of action."

"Yes. A course of action."

*****

"We got your truck back for you, Jimmy. But ain't a soul around to give us any answers."

The next morning, Alex came by to update us on what had happened. Laura preceded him and the four of us drank coffee and ate cinnamon rolls from Dottie's while Alex explained what he knew. They'd raided the nursery, rounded up scores of undocumented immigrants and arrested the owners. But there were no hulks or white cars or drivers of white cars to be found.

"What did the owners tell you?" I said.

"Nothing we didn't already know. Some unknown entity, or group or network of people supply them with workers. Legal or illegal. But they don't know where they come from or who they are. They never asked questions and they had no answers."

"Yeah, sure. An unknown entity like Lon Claymore."

"We ain't got no evidence of that."

"That's ridiculous," I said. "There has to be a paper trail somewhere."

"Maybe so, but we ain't got no bead on it." He was out the front door when he turned back for a goodbye. "I'll keep you posted."

*****

"Tiresias has a girlfriend."

We all heard the scream from my terrace. Janie had come over earlier to do her chores as the four of us were deep in conversation, and now she came running in through the French doors. We looked up as she gestured wildly.

"Come. Come quick. You gotta see this. Tiresias has a girlfriend."

We followed her out, across the terrace and past Tiresias' sand pit to his hollowed out log he sleeps in.

"Look," she said, pointing next to the log. There was another Ornate Box Turtle about the same shoebox size as Tiresias, standing directly in front of him. They rubbed noses gently, oblivious to us.

"How do you know it's a female?" said Laura.

"It's just gotta be. Look at them kiss."

"They definitely are enjoying each other's presence," said Akira.

"Can't you prove it, Mr. O? I mean, don't male turtles have a, well, you know? And female turtles wouldn't have one. Right?"

"That's true, Janie, but that is actually very difficult to detect."

Which is true, because the penis is stored inside the male's tale and rarely seen, but the stronger truth was that I didn't particularly want to give turtle sex lessons to Janie.

"There's an easier way," I said. "Look here. See how large Tiresias' tail is and how his eyes are orange? But her tail is short and thin, and her eyes are a pale yellow. Definite differences in the male and female, so yes, she is without a doubt, a she."

"Wow. I never knew all that."

Whew. I'd hedged that birds-and-bees issue successfully.

While Janie bent over and examined their tails and eyes closely, Laura whispered to me out of the side of her mouth. "You just made that up didn't you, you sly Irish devil?"

"The truth. The whole truth and nothing but the truth," I said. And it was. But then, try and convince Laura of that.

Janie stood up. "Now that we know for sure, you have to decide what to call her. What would be a good name for her, Mr. O?"

"How about an ancient Greek name to go with Tiresias? Clytemnestra, maybe."

"Oh, no. She's the one in that Seamus Haney poem you gave me. The one who killed her husband. I think, instead, Lissie would be better."

Laura jumped in the discussion. "I don't seem to recall any Greek women named Lissie."

"It's short for Lysistrata. You know, the Greek woman that organized a sex strike against the men. Isn't that a great idea? A sex strike. Zoey was reading the play and told me all about it."

"Lissie it is then," I said, although I wondered what a fourteen year old would know about withholding sexual favors by going on strike.

"Well, gotta go. Oh, by the way, I really like that one poem in the book you gave me. The one about the cockroach and the moth. Can we discuss it the next time I come over?"

"Plan on it," I said. It would be better than dealing with the sex lives of turtles.

Later that night, Akira and I laid the ground work for, as we had called it, our course of action.

It was completely dependent on Laura.

24

Laura walked in to Advance Loans underdressed and over-wired.

She wore a dirty white shirt of mine that we tore the arms off of at the shoulders, dirty jeans with holes in the knees and pink flip flops, and her hair was stringy. She had a trashy appearance, if that is possible for Laura. There were enough wires under her clothing to mic an outdoor rock concert. She carried a weekly paystub for a woman who worked as a waitress at Dottie's, as well as a fake ID in the woman's name, too.

Akira and I sat in my pickup across the street a half a block down, listening, along with a recording device.

"You think she will be alright?"Akira said. He had traced Toshi to Advance Loans a few days earlier when I had been dealing with the two hulks.

"I'd be more comfortable if there was two way communication," I said. "But this will have to do." We watched as the smoked glass front door ate her up and she disappeared inside. We heard nothing but silence.

"I don't think it's working," I said.

Then a ding sounded, like a small countertop hand bell you'd ring for help.

"How I help you?" A male voice, with a heavy Asian accent spoke, and I gave a sigh of relief.

"Yeah," said Laura, putting on a little accent of her own. "Heard you people give quick cash. I gotta have cash and I gotta have it fast. Like now, or sooner."

"How much you need?"

"Five Hunerd."

"That's lot money. You fill out paper first."

After a few minutes of silence, other than rustling papers and a presumed ID showing, the conversation resumed.

"Say here on paper, you work waitress. Yes?"

"Yep. Here's my pay stub for last week. I get this much each week, plus what I make in tips, so it ain't gonna be no trouble paying you back."

"Okay, you sign here."

I looked at Akira. "They make it about as easy as taking a leak to get a loan."

"Taking a leak?" he asked.

"It means... I'll explain later," I said. The electronic conversation started again.

"Here you money. Pay back in two week. This much."

"That's a lot of money to pay back in two weeks," said Laura, feigning surprise in her voice. "What kind of interest you guys get?"

"Standard amount. Thirty percent."

"Hey. Ain't that against the law? They got what they call usury laws or something, you know."

"You want money? That's deal. If no, you go someplace else."

"Yeah, yeah, yeah."

"Pay back, two week, or else."

"Or else what?"

"No good for you."

Laura emerged from the smoked glass door a minute later, walked down the street away from us, and we picked her up around the corner, as planned. She hopped in and the three of us sat crowded on the bench seat of my truck.

"As you could probably tell from the voice, that was not your son, Toshi. But I was being watched through what was obviously a two way mirrored window, and I could hear movement from at least one other person in the backroom. Maybe Toshi."

"I say we give it a little more time," and I repositioned the truck so we could observe the front door again.

"How was my accent?" said Laura.

"You not only looked trashy, you sounded trashy. Face it, you're a natural."

She shot me a dirty look. "How can these guys get away with a scam like this? Thirty percent."

"People like you," I said. "Desperate people," and I laughed.

"It's not funny."

"No, you're right. It isn't funny."

"Okay," said Akira, "what is this saying about taking a leak?"

Laura looked over at me, past Akira. "Say, what kind of English are you teaching him?"

"Practical stuff. Everyday expressions he can use."

She just shook her head.

"It means," I said to Akira, "to go to the bathroom. You know, number one."

"What's number one?"

Laura laughed. "You're just getting in deeper, O'Reilly."

At that moment, someone came out the front door of Advance Loans, turned and walked away from us. He wore black jeans and a black tee shirt, and had the tattoos scrolling down his arms. It looked like Toshi, but I couldn't tell from the back and at that distance, although it looked like one hand was bandaged.

Akira confirmed it. "That is him. My son, Toshi."

He got in a late model car and we followed him to a house on South Elizabeth Street. It was one of those cookie-cutter, one floor houses built in the early seventies. When he got out, he hitched his jeans up, put on sunglasses, picked up a billy club from the car and held it in his hand with a stub of a bandaged pinkie. He walked up to the front door and banged on it with the club.

"I do not think this looks good," said Akira.

"No, indeed," said Laura.

When the door opened, Toshi placed his body in the opening and then shot inside, forcing his way in, past someone. The door closed.

"So," I said, "I guess your son is the local loan shark enforcer for the Yakuza."

"What do you think we should do?" said Laura.

We gave it a minute, and then moved fast. When we burst through the front door, Toshi was in the act of beating an elderly man with the billy club. Two small children, possibly grandchildren, hid behind a couch.

I threw a cloth laundry sack over Toshi's head and shoulders, and Akira and Laura helped disable him before he knew what hit him.

After we hog-tied him and put him in the cab space behind my truck seat, I went back in the house. The old man had sustained a couple of blows. I bent over him to see how bad he was. The kids peeked out from behind the couch.

"It's going to be okay," I said to them. I dialed 911 on a wall phone and called it in as a B and E with assault without giving my name. I turned back to the kids as I walked out the front door.

"An ambulance and the police will be here in a few minutes. You don't have to be afraid. Everything is going to be just fine." Although I knew it wasn't. A kid couldn't witness something like that and be just fine.

147

"The old man will be okay," I told Laura and Akira at the truck. "The kids are terrified, though."

"Maybe we should stay with them," said Laura.

"Ideally, yes. Practically, no." Sirens already sounded in the distance. "Jump in. We've got to go. Now."

Laura looked over her shoulder at the front door as I pushed her in the truck after Akira. Toshi hollered all the way to the brownstone on Douglas. He kept screaming not to kill him. That he had not betrayed anyone. That he was loyal to the Yakuza.

Laura pointed to Akira and whispered. "He hasn't said anything yet. He," she pointed back to Toshi, "doesn't know it's us that nabbed him."

"Let him keep thinking it's his own people after him," I whispered back, under Toshi's screams. "Let him be terrified for awhile."

"Listen O'Reilly. I have to get out of these clothes."

I looked over at the dirty, sleeveless shirt, torn jeans and pink flip-flops. "Why Laura, you are the height of fashion. You ought to be on the cover of Vogue."

"I'm not kidding. These things are driving me crazy. I itch all over."

"Okay, okay. But we've got a stop to make first."

Toshi had pretty much lost his screaming voice by the time we arrived at the brownstone, hauled him up the back steps and propped him up in a chair. He kept whining in a hoarse voice, though.

"I didn't betray. I didn't betray. Loyalty. Loyalty. I am loyal. I swear."

"Looks like they scared the shit out of you," I said, as Laura and Akira untied and lifted off the cloth sack."

"You again," he said. When Laura untied his hands and came around to the front of the chair, he said, "You? From the loan? What are you doing here?" But when Akira joined us and faced him, his eyes got wide. "Father. You must leave. It is your fault. Look at this." He held up his hand with the bandaged finger. "Next, they will kill me. Go away. Leave me alone. They think I am betraying them. They will kill me."

The three of us pulled up kitchen chairs and sat in a semi-circle in front of him. For the first time, I got a close look at his tattoos, at least the ones on his arms. There were dragons and bamboo and other beasts and characters.

Akira saw me staring. "These, what you call tattoos, are *irezumi*. His Yakuza patrons have probably paid for all of this. He has, fifteen, maybe twenty thousand dollars worth of *irezumi* on his body."

"That's a lot of ink," I said.

"A lot of needle pricks, too," said Laura.

"He has dragons for power. Foo Dogs for protection. Characters from Suikoden, a book about outlaws. So, you see, my son believes he is an outlaw who needs power and protection."

"Why the three numbers?" I pointed to the numbers 8, 9 and 3 on the inside of one arm.

"In Japanese, eight is *ya*, nine is *ku*, and three is *sa*."

"Oh," said Laura. "Yakuza. Eight, nine, three. But what's the connection?"

"Yes. Yakuza. There is a card game called *Oicho-Kabu*, and in this card game eight, nine and three is the worst possible losing score. Yakuza believe they are the losers of society. My son believes he is a loser. How shameful." He looked directly at Toshi, and Toshi broke eye contact and lowered his head.

"Toshi, my son. What could take a hold of you to allow yourself to beat an old man like that?"

Toshi did not answer, but continued to look away.

"Do you know what these people you work for do? Do you know what happens to the children they take? To the women they take?"

149

Toshi nodded that he did, and then said, "They will kill me if I do not obey them. And they will kill me if I betray them by telling you what you are seeking."

"Let's get a few things straight," I said. "And let's lay down some ground rules. Here are the options we have. One, we can turn you over to the police and give them the recording we made from the Advance Loan transaction." His surprise registered at finding out we had recorded evidence. "Two, you can turn yourself in and offer testimony in exchange for protection. Or three, you can spill the beans to us right now and help Laura, your father and me."

"Spill the beans?" said Akira.

"Ah, another expression. Tell us everything," I explained.

"English sure is funny."

"I cannot do any of those," said Toshi.

Laura intervened. "You have no other options."

Toshi started to rise, but Akira was immediately behind him, forcing him back into the chair and holding him there, while Laura and I stood directly in front.

"The fact that my son is a coward is shameful enough." Akira talked about him in the third person, not acknowledging his presence. "But it does not alter the fact that he must pay for his actions."

"Three options," said Laura.

"What's it going to be?"

25

Mr. Fukumoto casually pointed to Toshi's bandaged stub of a finger.

"As you can see," he said, "those of us who commit even minor infractions, as well as those with whom we do business who do not live up to agreements, suffer certain fates."

"Is that a warning?" I said.

"Only an observation."

Mr. Fukumoto, a *wakagashira* or regional boss, was dressed in a black sharkskin suit, with a crisp white shirt and tie, and sported dark sunglasses that hid his eyes. His slicked back salt and pepper hair gave away his middle age, and belied his youthful look. I could see the edges of his *irezumi* peeking out the top of his collar on his neck. He sat, pokerfaced, licking an unlit cigar.

An Asian girl stood behind him, silent. She was in her twenties, but she was dressed as a school girl. She wore a white blouse and a short pleated skirt with knee socks, like a Catholic school girl would wear. And her jet black shoulder-length hair was separated in unbraided pigtails that stuck out on each side of her head and hung down. What a fantasy world these Yakuza live in, I thought.

Laura, who was dressed in one of her tony silk outfits, and I, sat across from him in a windowless room at an undisclosed location, undisclosed because Toshi had to bring us there blindfolded. Since I considered Toshi to be a reluctant accomplice at best, I convinced him I would be wired and transmitting, and he believed it. It would, I felt, keep him in line. In fact, I wasn't wired, and it was a good thing, because Laura and I were taken aside and frisked before we were given an audience with the *wakagashira*.

"I am happy to see," said Mr. Fukumoto, "that young Toshi, after his unfortunate finger lesson, is now not only a diligent and hard worker, but is taking the initiative to bring us new business."

After he dismissed Toshi with a wave of his hand, he raised the other hand, and School-Girl stepped forward, lit his cigar and stepped back.

"My business partner, Ms. Jones," I said, referring to Laura, "and I, myself, are-"

"The fact that you, Mr. Smith, and Ms. Jones here, wish to use false names is not a concern to me."

"Oh, but those are our real names," said Laura. I cringed. Her voice was overly sincere and completely unbelievable.

"Come now. We need no pretense here. Actually, Fukumoto is not my real name either. And believe me, if we need to know your actual identity, we will find that out, as well as how to find you, yourselves."

"Another warning?"

"Another observation. Now, let us get down to business. Toshi has said that you are in need of our services, and I accept you on good faith and his word. So, how may we help you?"

"We understand that you may be able to supply certain goods we need to acquire for business purposes," I said.

Laura continued the ruse. "Yes. Mr. Smith and I have been engaged in a number of business enterprises in western Kansas and would now like to expand into this area. We specialize in a certain type of clientele, and have a need for exclusively Hispanic merchandise."

"And what quantity of inventory do you need to stock?"

"We would like to start with ten units," I said, trying to match his objective description of pimping.

"Hispanic?" he said. "Sometimes we have to backorder for specialty items, but that is certainly doable from our end. And you are in luck. Quite often our inventory is shipped out quickly to such places as Bangkok, Manila and Seoul where there is high demand. But we currently are overstocked in the area you have interest. This is our price for that much inventory."

He wrote a figure on a slip of paper. School-Girl stepped forward again, turned the paper toward us and pushed it across the desk for us to read, then silently stepped back.

"That's a bit more that we had in mind," I said.

"The price is non-negotiable, except for the fact that we, ourselves, have a strong need for certain types of merchandise. Your firearm laws are much less restrictive than in our country, so we are always willing to bargain for large quantities of those."

"That is something Ms. Jones and I will have to discuss. We would, however, like to inspect the merchandise, and perhaps even choose from the stock you have on hand. Then we can discuss terms."

I could almost feel Laura cringing at discussing human flesh in terms of inventory and units and stock and price.

"If I can be more specific," said Mr. Fukumoto, "we refer to our merchandise as Comfort Workers, and we are in the business of Selling Spring. When we Sell Spring, we provide only the highest quality of Comfort Workers. Still, I understand your concern and desire to inspect the merchandise."

"One other issue," said Laura. "Our, ah... Comfort Workers have always joined our business willingly. How do we know these individuals will not simply leave us?"

"We have a training program that will provide you with persuasive techniques to use."

Mr. Fukumoto was making the business of prostitution sound like a franchise we were buying into, like a McDonald's or a Dairy Queen. I half expected him to have School-Girl pull out a company manual.

"Keep in mind, however, these individuals are what you call undocumented workers. The element of fear can do wonders for company morale," he said.

I could feel Laura heave a sigh of relief at this information. Not about the fear aspect, but about hearing the term undocumented workers, because we both now knew we were close to perhaps finding Maria, Inez Gonzalez' sister-in-law, as well as the other unfortunate women.

Mr. Fukumoto stood as School-Girl withdrew his chair and placed it against the wall.

"In order to inspect the available stock of Comfort Workers," he said, " you will be taken to our warehouse by a driver, which will necessitate your being blindfolded once again. I apologize for the inconvenience."

Such concern, I wanted to say, but bit my tongue instead.

*****

Laura and I stood, blinking our eyes and trying to adjust them to the intense sunlight after our driver removed the blindfolds. We had ridden in silence the entire trip.

There had really been no need for the blindfolds. We looked back inside the rear shell of the windowless van we'd been transported in, with its wooden benches attached to each side, and shackles that hung from the bulkhead.

Laura shook her head. "It looks like the Comfort Workers don't get to travel in too much comfort."

"At least they didn't shackle us," I said. "Hey Buddy, we could have done without those blindfold things."

Our driver shrugged his shoulders and said something in Japanese. Then he motioned us to follow.

"I don't think he understands English," said Laura.

I whispered to Laura. "That could just be a put-up job. I'll see if I can trick him into a response so we'll know for sure." Since Mr. Fukumoto didn't introduce us, I didn't have a name for him, so I just called out, "Hey Driver. You know what time it is?"

"Oh, that was clever," whispered Laura.

Driver mumbled something in Japanese.

"Just be careful what we talk about," she said. "I don't trust these guys."

"What? They're men of honor. You know the old saying. Honor among thieves."

"Yeah. More like honor among finger-slicers."

We looked around us as we walked toward a two-story, wood frame house that sat in a large swale with hills around it that blocked the view out. There were no visible landmarks for identification purposes. I had tried to identify sensory elements like sound and smell as we drove, but didn't pick up too many clues, other than a few sounds and feel for the time, which was about a forty-five minute drive. But then I hadn't known our starting point either. I looked up at the house and saw bars on the upstairs' windows.

"I'm a little worried about Toshi. Since they didn't let him drive us, maybe they suspect something. If they finger him-"

I winced at Laura's unfortunate choice of words.

"I mean, if they figure out he's helped us, it could be really bad for him."

"Don't worry. He's got seven more fingers and two thumbs."

She glared at me.

"Sorry. But he knew what he was getting into," I said.

A man with an automatic weapon stood guard on the front porch, exchanged words with Driver, and escorted us inside. Driver motioned us upstairs where the guard took a padlock off of a door, opened it and we all four entered a long extended room.

Immediately, a dozen or more women started pleading in Spanish, all at the same time and loudly. The guard lifted his weapon and there was instant quiet. I guess gun-in-the-air is the international sign for shut up.

I pulled out a pen and small note pad and fake-wrote in front of Driver's eyes. "Okay? Me write?"

He nodded yes, so I don't know if he understood the words or the pantomime. There were cots lining the sides of the room, each numbered, and each woman had stood before a cot when the guard motioned to them earlier. I counted nineteen women. I started taking notes, but it was mainly a front for looking for Maria, at least from what I remembered from Inez' photo. When I spotted her at the far end of the room, I wrote "Maria number 9" and showed it to Laura. She looked and nodded acknowledgement to me.

I knew I couldn't say anything to Maria, but I wrote *"Maria, pequeño Julio y Elena están bien."* That really taxed my Spanish capabilities and probably wasn't correct, but if I could get it to her, at least she would know Little Julio and Elena were safe. I made no mention of her husband's fate, though.

We passed Maria, reached the far end of the room and I stalled, making a show out of looking out the window. What I saw, surprised me. I could see above the surrounding hills that blocked our views below. There was still nothing to ID the place, landmark-wise. But there, out in an open field, was one of those trucks with a bright yellow sun and derrick silhouette on it. I knew there had to be some connection with Simpson Oil Company and Lon Claymore and all of this. This could be the break to make that connection.

I casually turned around, and sure enough, our two Yakuza lackeys were walking back to the door, backs to us. I slipped the note to Maria and when I looked back over my shoulder, she stared at me with pleading eyes, but there was nothing more I could do at this point, other than inform her and hope that it gave her some consolation.

Back in the van, Driver drove us out the gravel entrance, up and through the obscuring hills, and then suddenly came to a stop. He realized he'd forgotten to put the blindfolds back on us, not that they were needed. But when he came around, opened the side van door and handed us the blindfolds, I looked out and picked up on at least one landmark. At the entrance to this place, wherever it was, a marker stood. A limestone rock marker with kanji carved into it. I memorized the kanji for future reference, and then slipped the blindfold on as he watched.

26

"So, what the Hell is our next move?"

Akira, Laura and I sat in my living room, discussing what to do next, after Laura and I had been unceremoniously dumped off by Driver next to my truck where Toshi originally met us in downtown Wichita.

"You got me," said Laura.

Akira had a far-off look. "It seems to me..."

The phone rang.

"I assume you are satisfied with the available merchandise?"

It was Mr. Fukumoto. I wasn't expecting a call and certainly wasn't ready to deal with him yet. I turned to Laura and Akira and mouthed his name.

"Yes," I answered confidently. "You have excellent Comfort Workers."

"Please, on the phone, let us use more objective terms. Merchandise."

"Yes, your merchandise is excellent." I rattled off ten of the women's numbers, making sure I included Maria's, and told him this was the specific stock we wanted.

"Good. Then in payment, we would need the following." He went down an itemized list of firearms that included scores of automatic and semi-automatic handguns as well as assault rifles. Strange, considering he didn't want to get specific with the other merchandise. "How soon could we conclude our business?"

"I'll need at least three days." I stalled for as much time as possible.

"Two days. No more than that. If you need to, I am sure you can do a straw buy. I will be in contact." He abruptly hung up.

I turned to Laura and Akira, showing them the list. It included everything from Smith and Wessons, to Rugers, Glocks, Berettas and SIG Sauers. "He is giving us two days and said to do a straw buy."

"What's that?" said Akira.

"It's when a middleman makes a purchase from a legal vendor, but illegally passes it on. What are we going to do?"

"Go to the authorities with what we know and let them take over," said Laura.

"Not a good idea." Akira and I blurted it out in unison.

"First," I said, "what is it that we know? The Japanese Mafia is in possession of nineteen illegals, all women, and they want a shit-load of firepower in exchange for them. Second, what is it that we don't know? A, where the Japanese Mafia is located. B, how to get in touch with them. C, how to get in touch with our one contact or where Toshi's current location even is. And D, where the women are located."

Akira jumped in with a follow-up. "If you go to the police with such an imbalance of information, we are at a big disadvantage."

Laura countered. "If we do go to them, then set up an exchange of women for firearms, even though there will be no actual firearms, the authorities can monitor it, intercede and arrest the Yakuza at the exchange."

Akira and I looked at each other, amused at such naiveté. He decided to field this one, too.

"Dear Laura. You must understand that the Yakuza would never allow themselves to be put in such a position. Every precaution would be taken by them, every condition dictated, every step, ah...danced..."

"Choreographed?" I offered.

"Yes. Thank you. Choreographed. You cannot win."

"A better alternative," I said, "would be to find the women, release them, turn them over to the authorities, and then wait for the Yakuza to come after us. That way, the authorities will be in a position to protect us."

"Great. And just where and how are we going to find the women? We haven't got a clue as to where they are," said Laura.

"*Au contraire, mon chéri.* We have several clues. Slight as they may be."

"Drum roll please. And the clues are..."

"Yes," said Akira. "What clues?"

"First-"

"Cut all this first, second and A, B, and C crap. What are the friggin' clues?" Laura was getting impatient.

"We know it was about a forty-five minute ride to the house where the women are."

"From where? We don't even know from whence we started, O'Reilly."

"From whence?"

"If you can say *mon chéri*, Mr. Smarty-pants, I can say from whence."

"Okay. Calm down, Laura. We don't know from whence we started. I'll grant you that."

Akira's head was going back and forth between us like he was watching a tennis match.

"But we do know we passed the airport. I heard the jet noise overhead. So we went west out of town-"

160

"Hold your horses right there. How do you know it wasn't McConnell Air Force Base on the east side of town, twenty miles in the other direction?"

I had to stop and think. She had me there. "All right, so we either went east out of town, or we went west out of town."

"Well, that really narrows it down, doesn't it, Smarty-pants?"

"Wait. It had to be west. Those big tankers have a whole different sound to them than commercial airliners. West. It was definitely west."

"So, you've narrowed it down to the west half of Sedgwick County. Let's see. That is only approximately five hundred square miles. What's your next move?"

"My next move?" I had to think fast trying to recall the sensory information I'd taken in on my blindfolded trip. "The laughter. Didn't you hear the laughter when we passed it?"

"Laughter? That's great, O'Reilly. Now we just look for a house with a continuous party with lots of laughter somewhere past the airport, and we're home free."

"Not a party. It was the Gibbons at Tanganyika. Those wild primates that screech and hoot out that crazy laughter sound. We had to be passing close to the Tanganyika Wildlife Park."

Laura thought for a minute as Akira studied her. "You may actually have something there, O'Reilly."

"Think about it. No more than ten or twelve minutes later we pulled up to the house, and it was almost all on dirt roads. You could feel it. So we weren't traveling farther west on the highway. Look. I drew the kanji out I'd memorized from the stone at the front of the house's driveway. This is how we find the house."

Akira looked at them. "Yes. Three kanji. All numbers. Eight, nine and three."

"Ya, ku and sa. Yakuza," I said.

161

"One more little detail," said Laura. "If, by some miracle we should happen to stumble on this house, how do we free nineteen women and transport them safely out of their guarded premises and away from these thugs? Minor detail, I know. Just asking."

"Hey. This is a work in progress."

27

Our rented cargo van sat parked a quarter of a mile up the road from the Yakuza house. We were putting the finishing touches to Laura's question about one more little detail. Our carefully planned search and grab mission, with all the logistical elements mapped out and every contingency addressed.

Actually, we had no idea what we were doing.

Laura still wanted to go to the authorities. Akira wanted to simply walk up to the house alone, with us holding back, hidden. I preferred a full rear assault from the cover of the hills behind the house.

We were in a tight spot, time-wise. Our first day of the two that Mr. Fukumoto had allotted us was eaten up with van rental, bickering about tactics and endlessly driving the back roads looking for the house, with no success. Day two was more driving and search failure, until early afternoon, when I spotted a utility truck with a Simpson Oil logo on it and recalled what I'd seen from the window upstairs. We followed it, and sure enough, it led us right past the house, past the Yakuza stone at the entrance, before it turned into an easement access on the property. But day two was passing quickly, and Mr. Fukumoto's deadline approached.

In the end, Laura and I hid behind the hills to one side of the house, she with her Aikido stick and me with my Ruger, peering over the tops of the hills and down at the house. Akira drove the van up the drive and parked in front, in full view.

A guard walked out, holding his automatic weapon, and faced Akira, who simply had his Aikido stick slung over his back.

"Here we go, Laura. Either Akira pulls off one of the best dekes ever and makes this guy think he's one of them, or we are up shit-creek."

"I love it when you talk dirty," she said, staring straight ahead.

The two conversed in Japanese, and then both walked into the house. I turned to Laura. "See? I told you. Piece-a-cake."

Then we heard a scream.

"Piece of cake?" she said. "I think you forgot the frosting." We went running down the hill, each with Aikido stick and Ruger in hand, respectively, and burst through the front door. Not a particularly wise tactic, but a spur of the moment reaction nonetheless.

Luck was with us. Akira stood over the unconscious guard. He wiped a small bit of blood from his Aikido stick, while the guard, laying on the floor, had blood trickling from one ear.

"A purely defensive move," he said, and then smiled.

"I think the cake's just been frosted," I said.

Akira hoisted the guard over his shoulder and carried him upstairs. He had incredible upper body strength. Laura took the padlock off the women's' holding room, and when we entered, guard in tow, shrieks started flying. When I held my Ruger up, they all got quiet and lined up by their beds.

I hated using intimidation, but I'd been right. That was the international sign for shut up.

"Does anyone speak English? *¿Habla Inglés?*" They all shook their heads, no. I looked at Maria, but spoke to everyone, hoping my Spanish was intelligible. *"No hay peligro. Vengan con nosotros."* It must have been, because they all followed me out, while Akira took the guard's cell phone and locked him in the room.

The van ride to downtown Wichita was almost riotous, if not comic. Nineteen women packed into the back of an extended cargo van, all talking in Spanish at once, with Maria pleading for information about her family and me not knowing how to communicate much else, other than what I'd already told her. Laura on her cell phone calling WPD, telling them what we were bringing them and that they needed to contact ICE. Akira combing the contacts on the guard's phone and shouting excitedly when he found a number for Toshi. It was the most animated I'd ever seen him, and the entire van was near bursting its seams with confusion and excitement.

*****

Celebratory picnic time ensued in my back yard the next day.

It was a celebration tempered with some sober realities. We celebrated the safe release of the women, as well as the previous safe return of the children. But this was tempered with the realization that twenty-seven men had died, and the fact that all the women and children, although united and safe, would most certainly be deported back to Mexico. Also, if I had known what was yet to come, the occasion would not have been a celebration.

For the moment, though, we were all happy. I fixed fried free-range chicken from a local farmer and baked beans for the picnic, while Laura brought potato salad and Akira concocted two different iced teas. One, green tea with a fresh woodsy aroma and taste, and two, an oolong variety that was sweet and fruity, with a honey bouquet.

Janie and her mother Francine joined us, and brought their dog along to keep my box turtles company. While we pigged out on crispy chicken and side dishes and compared the taste of Akira's two iced teas, we watched W.B. go nose to nose with Tiresias and Lissie.

With the weather change, the day was cool and breezy, and the sun's brightness seemed to light the world with a special glow. It put a yellow-white tinge to everything, one that said all would be well.

While Francine and Laura demanded to take care of cleanup duties, and Akira crouched in fascination watching the turtles and puppy do their playful dance, Janie sat next to me on the terrace and squinted at me.

"I really like the poems that Archy the cockroach writes," she said. "They're kind of hard to understand without any punctuation, but they're really neat."

"Glad you're enjoying them." I squinted back, unconsciously.

"I don't get the one called 'the lesson of the moth,' though. I mean, this moth tells Archy he'd rather be happy for like a millisecond by the excitement of flying into fire and dying, rather than living forever and being bored. It doesn't make sense."

"Maybe it's kind of like you and Zoey," I said.

"Yeah. Zoey does crazy things on the spur of the moment without thinking, just like the moth does. She has a great time, but she's always regretting it afterwards. But me, I'm not like the moth, and I'm not bored or anything."

"No, but you are more practical. You can be practical without being bored."

"I guess that's true. But still, just like Archy says, it would be cool to want something as badly as the moth wants to fry himself."

I started to ponder the implications of that thought and how it pertained to my life, when Akira's giggles interrupted me. Loud giggles. Laura and Francine came out from the kitchen to see what was going on. Janie started laughing, herself.

Akira kneeled in the grass, his eyes shut tight, and he covered his mouth with one hand as he giggled so hard his shoulders shook. W.B.'s big pink tongue lapped wildly at one of Akira's ears, slobbering one whole side of his face. Tiresias and Lissie each crawled up Akira's separate thighs, their necks outstretched, curious to find out what was happening.

"Janie, I think the sight of this beats flying into a flame and becoming a cinder any day."

It was a perfect moment in a perfect day.

After Laura left to teach a late afternoon class at WSU, and Janie, Francine and W.B. packed up to go home, I pondered how to get Akira back to his place. Would he magically disappear and materialize at the Cimarron Breaks, or did I need to offer to drive him there?

That's when the phone rang. I started to pick up, when Akira whipped out the cell phone from the Yakuza house.

"Didn't you turn that over to the authorities yesterday?" I said.

"I think it slipped my mind." He grinned.

"Slipped your mind?"

"It's my only possible connection to Toshi. The only way I may still be able to find him again."

By then, the call had gone to voice mail. Then a text came through. It read: Voice mail code, 8316.

We looked at each other and then he madly punched in the code to retrieve voice mail. When it came on, I recognized Mr. Fukumoto's voice.

"Unfortunately for you, we have visited the house before the police you sent arrived. Unfortunate, for there will be retributions. Oh yes, if you would like to see your friend Toshi again, you will find directions at Gate C." He named the meat processing plant where I'd followed the white car to.

Akira followed the redial prompt, but a stilted, automated voice said, "This number no longer in service."

28

Gate C was padlocked from the inside, but a sealed envelope had been wedged in between a galvanized post and the attached chain link. Mr. Smith was written on the outside along with the three Japanese kanji for eight, nine and three.

I ripped open the envelop and we both read the note inside: Mr. Smith (O'Reilly), You have erred badly. You may meet your friend by following the railroad tracks at the west side of this plant and look for number 493752.

Akira and I looked at each other, and then tore out running west to the tracks.

"What is this number? What does it mean?"

"I have no idea," I said, as we scanned the west side of the plant looking for numbers and entrances, and then scores of smaller, separate storage buildings and their numbers. Nothing correlated. I turned around in frustration and that's when I saw it.

Box cars. Lines of boxcars, each with an individual six digit number. We ran down one line of cars looking at numbers but found no match. We crawled between two cars, over the heavy, metal coupling mechanism and draft gear, to the next track and ran back up the line of cars. Half way there we saw the numbers. 493752.

It was a refrigeration car. The cooling unit at the rear of the car was running. When I pulled the lever on the

169

door and slid the massive panel open, large clouds of ice cooled air billowed out from the car, and we both coughed as it stung our lungs.

We had to wait for the clouds to dissipate, and then we stepped up on the metal foot rail and into the freezing cold of the boxcar. As the interior air cleared, we saw rows of butchered cattle carcasses, sides of beef suspended in the air. We weaved in and around them, pushing them apart to peer between.

Then, at the end of the row, we saw him. Toshi. His stiff body hanging from a meat hook, face and exposed arms, blue and iced over from the frozen air.

Akira embraced him at the waist, lifted his body up and off the hook, and laid him gently on the boxcar floor. Then he sat seiza, next to Toshi's corpse.

*****

After Toshi's bagged body had been removed, after the Crime Scene van had left and after homicide finished questioning us, Akira stood outside of the death car, staring at it for a long time.

His face was impassive, yet the pain beneath was evident. He dropped down in seiza, and brought his hands together at his heart and prayed. When he raised his head, for lack of anything else to say, I said, "Praying helps."

"Not praying," he said. "This is *gassho*."

"What's that?"

"*Gassho*. It means, two hands coming together."

"Same thing," I said.

"Same thing. But different."

He stood and I put a hand on his shoulder.

"This is my fault," he said.

"You can't blame yourself for choices that Toshi made."

"No. Still, it is my fault."

There was nothing more to say. We walked in silence back to my truck.

*****

A knife and a string rested on my reading room table. The small box they came in, left on my front porch, sat next to them.

"I don't get it," I said.

"*Yubizume*," Akira said. "If the Yakuza hands a man a knife and a string, it means they expect you to cut off the first part of your little finger."

"Oh, like that's going to happen."

"The knife is for the cutting. The string is to slow the bleeding. Toshi would have had to do that to himself, too."

"So, putting me through self-induced excruciating pain is supposed to settle the score? That's what these Yakuza guys think?"

"No. It weakens you. Symbolically. In the old days, when a Samurai sword was gripped properly, the little finger was the strongest. It controlled the movement of the entire sword. If you lost a portion of your little finger, then you lost that control, and you became dependent on the master for protection. Today, they are more or less just making a point."

"A point well taken, but I think I'll pass on this one." I picked up the objects and tossed them in the trash.

"You realize, of course, they will find you and do it themselves at their convenience."

It was a chilling thought.

"Well, I'll put it at the bottom of my to-do list."

171

29

The Yakuza didn't wait long to play their finger game.

Akira and I spent the next few days awaiting the release of Toshi's body, making funeral plans, keeping an eye out for the finger snatchers and making plans for what we would do next. He went with me on a skip trace job for Bomber Jackson and learned a little of what I do to actually earn a living.

We were vigilant, but when the Yakuza struck, it was still a surprise. In fact, I kept thinking of Cato in the Pink Panther movies, and how he would always jump out and attack Inspector Clouseau unexpectedly. I kept expecting some Cato character to pop out of nowhere and come slashing at me with a little finger knife.

We'd had just finished dinner at Latte Dottie's, and that turned out to be a surprise in itself. I'd forgotten that Lon Claymore was making a campaign stop in Chisholm, and when he and his entourage swooped down on the town and into the cafe, everyone came to life.

Part of the surprise was that Charlene was at his side, giving the impression of the ever-obedient wife. Baxter and crew were outside, standing guard on the sidewalk on Commercial Street, and Lon and Charlene walked through the door of Latte Dottie's, smiling and shaking every hand in sight. The local Wichita media followed him in with TV cameras being stuck in everyone's face.

They missed us, since we sat at the counter, our backs to them. But when Charlene noticed me out of the corner of her eye, she quickly turned and looked the other way. I nudged Akira.

"Let's get out of here before I make a fool out of myself on TV again," I said, and we snuck out the front door amidst all the hullaballoo, zipping past Baxter before he could think of anything to say. I couldn't resist a parting shot, however, back over my shoulder.

"How are the groin muscles doing?" I said, and Akira and I rounded the corner and started the several blocks walk back to my bungalow.

We were about half way there when Fukumoto's lackeys made their grab. A car pulled up next to us, its door flung open and we were both yanked inside and gone before you could say Jack Rabbit. Not exactly the Cato Pink Panther move, but startling, nonetheless.

The next thing I knew, we were sitting at a small wooden table in an abandoned outbuilding a few miles outside of Chisholm. They didn't even bother to blindfold us. That was of some concern. Did they have no plans to return us alive? Three young men in black slacks and black tees stood around us with their arms folded, *irezumi* blazing out from under the sleeves and down to the wrists.

I stared at their *irezumi*. "Hey Guys, I wish I'd known about the fad. I could have made a fortune in ink futures." They stood, stone-faced. No sense of humor.

Fukumoto walked in and stood before us. Akira stared at him, the man who was undoubtedly responsible for Toshi's murder, but said nothing. He stared at him impassively. Then Fukumoto nodded, and one of the young ones placed a knife and string on the table in front of me.

"I appreciate the opportunity," I said. "It's just that I'm not into self-mutilation. Never appealed to me, for some reason."

"You may be a man and pay your debt to us, or you may be a coward and let us do it for you."

"This sort of thing never really has caught on here in the States. The ladies just don't care for the look, if you know what I mean."

"You are being very... what is your word for it? Cavalier? And I am growing impatient, Mr. O'Reilly."

"Yeah? Well, why don't you take a long walk off a short pier?"

Fukumoto stepped toward me impulsively, and then thought better of it. He stepped back, got control of himself, nodded at the three hoods and they came at me. One held me down by the shoulders. Another splayed my fingers of the left hand out flat on the table and a third picked up the knife.

"Hey, come on Guys. Enough's enough, already."

Knife-boy, without so much as a How-do-you-do, raised the knife and brought it down in one swift motion. I closed my eyes and tightened my muscles, bracing for the pain.

I felt a finger bone fly up and hit me in the face, except there was no pain. Had I lost all feeling? Would the pain overwhelm me shortly?

I opened my eyes and instead of a finger bone, a wooden chip from the table was in front of me. My pinkie was intact and I let out a long, protracted breath.

"You do have one other option," Mr. Fukumoto said. "You may keep your precious finger and the women will continue to adore you."

"You don't have to be sarcastic about it. And what does that one other option entail?"

"Simply arrange a meeting between myself and your friend, Senator Claymore."

"He's no friend of mine," I blurted out. But then I thought, what would Fukumoto want in a meeting with him? "Lon Claymore? Why?"

"The reason does not concern you at this point. And friend or not, you have the ability to make the arrangement. Should you need justification to convince him, simply say we have a business proposition in regards to an upcoming event. You may offer this document as an inducement." He handed me a sealed envelope. "Please do not unseal it."

Akira, who had remained silent up until now, suddenly said, "*Sokaiya*."

Fukumoto's head snapped to Akira, and I said "What?"

"*Sokaiya*. It means, shareholders' meeting man. A famous Yakuza trick is to buy shares in a company and then blackmail them by threatening to disclose damaging information about the company at their next stockholder meeting."

"Your friend, whoever he is, is quite knowledgeable," said Mr. Fukumoto. "Just understand, it is better if you know no more."

Apparently, Fukumoto had no idea that Akira was Toshi's father, and this, as Martha Stewart would say, is a good thing. And this whole Yakuza-Claymore situation could be a good thing, too. At the very least, it was getting interesting.

"I'll see what I can do," I said.

"You will succeed. Keep your little finger in mind."

*****

A short time later, they dumped us off back at Latte Dottie's. The campaign glitz was still in full swing, and although the media had left, I could see Lon through the plate glass window, backslapping, handshaking and smiling until his teeth hurt. I started to go in, but Baxter blocked the door.

"I need to talk with Lon," I said.

"He doesn't want to see you."

"You haven't asked him yet."

"Standing order."

I was beginning to regret my earlier groin comment. Then, Akira gently put his hand on Baxter's arm and Baxter's eyes got wide as he seemed to involuntarily move out of my way. Aikida move or Reiki or whatever, I don't know and I didn't ask.

I pulled the envelope out and started to enter Dottie's, but two more suits stepped in front of me and whisked the envelope out of my hand, giving it to Baxter.

"What's this?"

I figured I wasn't going to get past all these goons in suits, so I just leveled with him. "A man by the name of Mr. Fukumoto says he needs a meeting with your boss and that the contents of that envelop will explain everything."

"I'll see that he gets it."

"I'd like to give it to him myself."

"I said, I'll see that he gets it."

"You'd better. It's a matter of finger-honor."

*****

I assumed the envelope was delivered and the meeting arranged, because my finger remained intact. At least for the next few days.

Cremation arrangements for Toshi had been made with Chisholm's mortuary, Watson Funeral Home, and I was surprised that Sam Watson had agreed to some of Akira's unusual requests and explicit instructions. Our plan was to receive the cremated remains and take them to the Cimarron Breaks, to put as much distance and time between me and the Yakuza as we could. Although, as

Akira said, if they wanted to find me, they would. What I hadn't counted on was the elaborate ceremonial aspects involved. I had assumed we would simply be handed the ashes.

Sam greeted us in the lobby, and instead of ushering us into a viewing room to transfer the ashes to us, he took us back into the working areas of the mortuary. Sam is short and thin, and always looks a little strange as he peers at you through his pince-nez glasses.

"Follow me, if you will, gentlemen. Excuse all the tools and equipment. The last few days have been quite busy." He took us to a workroom of gleaming metal, where Toshi's cremated remains were spread out on a long stainless steel tray. "Take as much time as you need, gentlemen." Then, he handed Akira an urn, left us alone and closed the door.

Akira went through several rituals involving incense, green tea and a rosary of sorts that he had brought, and he read a sutra. But then he pulled out two pairs of chopsticks and handed me one.

"Here. You must help me put the bone fragments from this tray into the container."

"I can't use these things."

"Do your best. Please. This is necessary. We begin at this end with the feet and work our way up toward the head. That way, he will not be upside down in the container."

I awkwardly began picking up pieces of Toshi and slowly transferred them to the urn. Akira extended his chopsticks to mine as we held the same bone fragment and I immediately withdrew my hand.

"You said never to do that. Remember, in the restaurant."

"This is the one time it is allowed. In fact, it is a necessary part of our custom. So, now you see why it would offend someone if you touched chopsticks while eating. They would be reminded of a loved one who is dead."

When we finished, he carefully wrapped the urn in a white cloth and we took it back to my bungalow for transportation to the Cimarron Breaks the next day.

30

We sat on the plateau at his place, looking out over the Cimarron Breaks, Laura, Akira and me. The urn rested at an outdoor alter near us with several coins next to it.

We had waited for Laura to teach a morning class and then all traveled the back roads through open country, Laura in her red Vette and Akira and me in my truck.

"This is the first of seven days of tribute for my son. Normally, his ashes would be interred in a family tomb. But here, I will scatter them in these hills, when the seven days end. The coins are to pay for his passage, as he must cross a river to his place of rest."

Kind of like the ancient Greek myth and the River Styx, I thought.

We sat in silence under a cool dome of blue sky, listening only to the Kansas wind whipping through the grasses and gullies. A long time passed and I can only speak for myself, but I felt at peace. At home, as if I belonged to the land itself, and Akira's admonition of letting go of the past seemed like it might be something achievable. Not only in regard to my deceased wife, Sondra, but in relation to my entire past. The violence that has followed me and plagued me. Maybe I could escape it.

Akira broke the silence. "Can you see them?"

"See who?" I said.

179

"They are out there. Can you not see them?"

Laura and I both looked out to the Breaks, then off to our sides and around behind us.

"There's no one there," said Laura.

"Out there, in the fields." He pointed off in the distance where empty rangeland, slopes and bluffs were all we saw.

"There's nobody there. Who are you talking about?" I said. I thought maybe he was having a mystical vision or something about Toshi and his relatives.

"The buffalo."

"Buffalo? I think you're losing it Akira. We're in the middle of the Breaks, but there are no buffalo out there. Just empty space, maybe a jack rabbit or two and a few bull snakes."

"I see fields full of buffalo. Dead buffalo. There are thousands of them. Their hides laid out to dry and their skulls and bones stacked high in pile after pile, as far as I can see."

I thought back to the stories I'd heard about the eighteen-seventies when the buffalo hunters came and slaughtered herds west of the Arkansas River. One picture I'd seen showed a hunter sitting on top of a pile of forty thousand hides, baled and ready to be shipped out. Forty thousand. It was done in the name of commerce, but with the silent consent of the government that looked the other way, knowing that wiping out the buffalo would also end the Native Americans' livelihood. A path to their extinction, too.

"You're living in the past," I said. But I wondered what sense of internal sight Akira must possess to see such a vision.

"Maybe," he said. "But they are there, nonetheless. So much needless death."

More fields of death, I thought. Everywhere I turned, there were fields of death. Even the past contained

180

them. We sat for a long time in the presence of death, both human and animal.

Finally, Laura rose and said, "Boys, you'll have to excuse me. I have a class to teach tomorrow. Give the buffalo my best."

"Wait," I said. "I've had a vision of my own. Not mystical. Just a practical one. Here it is. The women are safe. The children have been rescued. And a lot of people died. Needless deaths, as you have pointed out, Akira. But we still don't know why any of this has happened."

Laura sat back down. "And you know the answer?"

"No, but I know it's all connected somehow. Lon. The Yakuza. There has to be some tie-in we are missing."

"I'm not so sure," said Akira. "If that were so, why would the Yakuza have had to force an arranged meeting with this Mr. Claymore?"

"True. And yet- I just have this gut feeling. We're missing something."

"We know one thing for certain," said Laura. "If the Yakuza plan is to blackmail Claymore, then they have something nasty and big on him."

"Or his company."

"If we can find out what that something is, that might be the link. It might lead us to what or who is behind all of this."

"The who is the big question. Who brings in the illegals? Is it the Yakuza? Is it Lon Claymore's people? Is it the two hulks and the white car driver? Or do they all work together somehow? Or is it someone we haven't even stumbled on yet? That's the real mystery."

"If the Yakuza are planning on using a public shareholder meeting as blackmail leverage, maybe it's Claymore that brings in the illegals. Maybe that's what they have on him."

Akira looked at Laura and then at me. "This mystery solving business is interesting, but it is not our place to avenge these deaths."

"What are you talking about?" I said, and pointed to the urn. "Your own son is dead because of this nonsense. Don't you want revenge?"

"Revenge serves no purpose. It is a useless emotion that only wastes *ki*. It would harm me more than the act itself."

"What about justice?" said Laura. "Justice for the victims?"

"Each person's actions will determine their own destiny. There is balance in the universe."

Laura and I looked at each other. "Wait a minute. We might have some basic philosophical differences here," I said. "But even you have to admit that those who have done wrong have to be dealt with. Otherwise, why would you carry that Aikido stick with you all the time?"

"Defense. My *jo* is for self-defense."

"That is true," said Laura. "But you are a Tendai priest."

"Yes. And for me, the First Noble Truth is that life is suffering. I must accept that."

"Okay," Laura continued. "But you also believe in selflessness. And in selflessness, you believe that you are everybody, not just your own self."

My mind was spinning. I had no idea what they were talking about. "I'm lost, you guys."

"I'm just trying to show Akira that he doesn't have to hide behind his beliefs to ignore justice." She turned back to Akira. "Compassion and benevolence toward yourself, to ease your own suffering, which is your duty, is also compassion and benevolence for others, because you are one with the universe."

"This is true."

I seized the opportunity. "Well then. We can all work together, can't we?"

Akira smiled at both of us. "All for one, and one for all?"

"Oh. He knows about the three musketeers. Yes. That's exactly it." I continued to run with the opening. "The three musketeers. Let's see. You would be Athos," I said to Akira. "Silent. Secretive. Noble. And Laura, you're Aramis, charming and elegant. And a womanizer. Well, in your case, a manizer. Younger men."

"So, that means you are Porthos," Laura said. "Loud, coarse and vain."

I groaned. "Ah, but also courageous and generous."

Akira jumped up, held up his *jo* like a sword and yelled at the top of his lungs to the open plains. "All for One. One for all. Yee-heee."

"Don't get too carried away with the macho act. We still have to figure out what to do," said Laura.

"I've got it. Laura, use your university research connections to find out what's going on with Claymore's company. All I got from my computer work was that his company went vertical and they're up to their ass in acquisitions. I'm going to go after Simpson Drilling. Every time I turn around, I see one of their trucks and I want to know what's up with that. Akira, you find out what the Yakuza are doing. Especially with their interest in Claymore." I felt like a quarterback barking route instructions to his receivers in a huddle. I wanted to say "Hike on twenty-three. Break." But I didn't.

Laura handed me her cell phone. "You just inherited this."

"No. Please, Laura. Don't do this to me."

"We have to have some way to communicate. I'll pick up a prepaid throwaway for myself at a convenience store and call you to give you the number."

183

"Anything but this. Even the briar patch, but not this."

" Briar patch? Just remember, you are loud, coarse Porthos, not Br'er Rabbit."

I took the phone. I knew she was right.

After she left, I turned to Akira. "How are you going to start on the Yakuza?"

"I'm not. I will start by helping you. The trucks you mentioned. I know where one is."

31

The sun and derrick logo, on the side of a white pickup, rested in a basin below a drop-off, two ridges west of Akira's place. We stood looking down into the basin where a lone worker appeared to be surveying and laying out stakes.

"This is not the truck I have seen coming and going. This is a new one."

"Well," I said, "What say I pretend I'm the landowner. If I can get by with it, maybe we can pump him for some information."

We descended down the side of the ridge, through scrub brush and cedars, and I called out to the worker as we approached.

"Howdy."

He came up from his leveling instrument on a tripod and looked our way. "Howdy, yourself."

"My foreman and me, we was just out checkin' fences. Thought I'd see how it's comin' along here."

"I'm busting my chops to get all the pads laid out. I think they should be in with the heavy equipment next week. Course, I don't make those decisions."

"I got you there. Tell me again, I keep forgettin' what they call this whole thing, this here... ah, you know...

"Fracking."

185

"That's it. Fracking. I don't know why I can't remember that."

"Most people just call them oil wells, and that's okay by us, what with all the environmentalists and tree huggers. We don't need to go stirring up controversy where it's not needed."

"No Sirree, bob-a-looee, you're dead right on that one."

Off in the distance a rooster tail of red dust puffed up behind a car coming across the field. Before we could say our goodbyes, a uniformed officer was getting out of the unmarked car, now parked next to us.

"What can I do for you boys?"

Somehow, I knew that my pretexting game was up, at least as the landowner. I shifted persona. "We're on a pilgrimage."

The worker looked at us strangely. "You mean you're not the owner?"

"You thought I was the owner?"

"You said-"

"Oh, no. No. We're on one of those fundraising walks across the state. You know, where people pledge-"

"What's that thing for?" The cop looked at Akira's Aikido stick slung across his back.

That's his walking stick," I said.

"Why don't you let him answer for himself?"

"Oh, he doesn't speak English very well."

The cop looked at Akira. Akira bobbed his head up and down. "Walk stick. Walk stick."

"Boys, this here is private land. I'm afraid you're going to have to come along with me. You go sit in the back of the squad car there, and you, give me that there walking stick."

As we climbed in the back of the cruiser, I heard the officer say something to the worker, who answered, "Sorry Pete, I thought he was the owner."

Pete shot back, "Don't go talking to strangers. You ought to know better."

Ten minutes later, we sat in a small cinderblock building in the middle of nowhere that had a generic sign on the outside that read POLICE. Pete walked around behind us busying himself with a coffee maker. "I need to see some ID, Boys."

"Could I ask who you are?" I said.

"I'm the law."

"Other than Pete, does the law have a name?" He didn't have a badge or name tag.

"Yep. Smith and Wesson." He patted his holstered side arm, which appeared to be an old Smith and Wesson .357 Magnum, otherwise known as the Highway Patrolman.

"That's kind of an antique."

"It gets the job done. Now, let's cough up some ID."

I put my billfold on the desk, and Akira pulled out his Non-Immigrant Visa card. Pete, or Smith and Wesson as he was now known, shuffled through them, and then said, "So, we got one private dick and one Chink."

"I prefer to be called a private investigator," I said. "And, ignoring the racist label you used, my friend is a Jap, not a Chink."

"Whatever. You boys make yourself at home in the cell over there. I got a few calls to make."

In the corner of the one room police station, if that's what it was, was a small barred enclosure, door open. We went in and sat down. I could hear Pete's voice as he tried to talk in muffled tones on the phone.

"O'Reilly and Sato. Said they're on a pilgrimage. Uh-huh. Uh-huh. That's what I thought."

A sinking feeling began to creep into my gut. It felt like one of those old Twilight Zone episodes where somebody's car breaks down in a small village where the residents walk around with zombie eyes and the person's car is found but the they are never seen or heard from again.

"I got a bad feeling about this, Akira."

He just nodded in agreement.

"Sorry I dragged you into this."

"No matter."

"Well, Boys, you might as well make yourselves comfortable. You're gonna be our guests for a few hours."

"What charge you holding us on, Smith? Or do you prefer Wesson?"

"Vagrancy."

"Vagrancy? We got ID. We got visible means of support. We got permanent residence."

"You from around here?"

"Not exactly."

"Vagrancy." He walked over and clanked the cell door shut.

I thought about trying to call Laura on the cell phone she'd left me, which Pete hadn't bother to search me for. But I didn't have a number for her, and I figured he'd hear me anyway and then confiscate it. Akira and I whispered back and forth for a short time.

"What's this fricking business about?" he asked.

"Fracking," I corrected him. "It's a method of extracting oil and gas from deep in the ground from shale deposits."

"And it is against the law?"

"No. It's legal. But it has the potential, among other harms, of groundwater contamination. And in some areas west of Wichita, that means possibly contaminating the Equus Beds. A major source of underground water."

Pete showed actual signs of life and got up from his desk. He walked to the only door, opened it and called back to us. "Gotta go out for a bit. Don't you Boys go nowhere, now." He let out a long, coarse laugh as he slammed the door behind him.

"Geeze. Everybody's a kidder," I said. Then we sat in silence for a long time. Suddenly, Laura's cell phone rang. I fumbled with it, but managed to connect.

"O'Reilly. I got a phone number for you. It'll be on your screen. It's my throwaway I bought."

"Thanks, Laura, but I gotta tell you, right now Akira and I are a little indisposed. We're sitting in a jail cell out in the middle of nowhere."

"What did you do now, O'Reilly?"

"There you go accusing me again. Nothing. We were just trespassing and pretexting by posing as a landowner and a foreman. Just misdemeanor stuff."

"For cryin'-out-loud, O'Reilly. You never learn. If you're in jail, then you haven't heard the news."

"What's that?"

"That Claymore company stockholder meeting the Yakuza wanted in on?"

"Wait. Let me put this on speaker so Akira can hear." I hunted around the keypad until I found what looked like a tiny speaker icon and pressed it. "Okay."

"That stockholder meeting was held this afternoon. Guess what? Claymore didn't bite on the blackmail threat, so this Yakuza goon released all this damaging information. The company's stock hit rock bottom."

"What kind of information?"

"Information like, in Pennsylvania where they had oil and gas leases, there was no safety oversight and a bunch of fracking wells wound up contaminating groundwater. That was bad enough. But then, they bribed several officials to hush it up, and now there's probably going to be a multimillion dollar class-action suit."

"Well, then they're doing the same thing here. That's what Akira and I were investigating. A fracking well. You got to get us out of here."

"You might be safer there. Since the Yakuza didn't get blood money out of Claymore, they're bound to come back to you for retribution."

"Holy shit." Just then I heard the crunch of tires on gravel outside. "The law has just returned. Gotta hang up."

"Where are you?"

But the door was opening, so I hit the end key and slid the phone back in my pocket.

A few hours later, as Akira and I dozed on our cell cots, I heard the metal latch clank open.

"Looks like you boys been sprung."

My mind jumped around. How could Laura have found us here? But when I looked up, it wasn't Laura. Instead, the two hulks stood staring at us. Bubba and the billy-club man.

"I'm remanding you to the custody of these gentlemen."

"Gentlemen? You're using the term a little loosely, aren't you?"

Bubba started toward me, but the other one held him back. "We'll have time for that later."

"This doesn't look too official," I said.

"Like I said, I'm the law, so that makes it official. Here's your ID back."

Akira walked over to the desk and pointed to his Aikido stick. "May I have my *jo*, please?"

Bubba picked it up and stared at it. It looked like a matchstick in his meaty hand. He started laughing hysterically, and then handed it to Aikira. "Sure. You bet. We'll have us some fun with this later."

For the second time, I was dumped in the back seat of the giant quad-cab truck with the elevated monster wheels.

32

"Hey, Bubba. Where you taking us?"

The truck zipped down a two lane blacktop, although I wasn't sure what direction we headed.

"Umm." Bubba appeared to be thinking really hard about the question. It was a tough one. "Salty, where are we taking them?"

"Shut up and don't use my name."

Bubba and Salty? This was getting more folksy by the minute. "Yeah, Salty, where are you taking us? " I said. "No place with corn kernels, I hope."

A long pause, and then Salty caved. I guess he thought he would show off his smart-ass attitude. "A little birdie told me you're interested in our operations, snooping around and all. So, we're going to take you on a little tour of the facilities."

"Yeah, huh." Bubba guffawed. "A tour. We're takin' you on a little tour."

It sounded like George and Lennie repartee from a Steinbeck novel.

Akira finally found his voice. "I wonder if you would mind stopping by my place. I would like to pick up a few things."

Nothing like being outrageous, I thought. I jumped in and played right along.

191

"Yeah," I said. "My camera, so we could take a few pictures of our tour. A little remembrance of all the fun we're going to have." If we could con them into it, maybe I could get to my Ruger in the cutaway of my truck.

Bubba started guffawing again, but Salty nudged him, whispered something, and then addressed Akira. "Where is your place?" I figured he thought maybe they would get something out of us there. We both had a mutual interest in the side trip.

But before Akira could tell him, Salty's phone rang. "Hello. Yep. Okay." A man of few words, he hung up. "Looks like you get your tour now." He turned to Bubba. "Boss says pronto."

Bubba guffawed again. "Pronto. You get your tour pronto."

It was dusk when the quad-cab turned off the two lane and crunched over gravel on a raised bed of a newly made entry way. I could see lights in the distance as we passed the shadowy landscape on each side, painted with dark red gulches, grainy irregular slopes and gray gypsum buttes of the Cimarron Breaks.

But what unfolded before us was an amazing sight. Here, in the middle of all this beauty was a giant raised pad of earth, perhaps two football fields in size, leveled, with its sides tapering off into the dark void of the Breaks. It looked like an oversized scar that had puckered up across someone's belly.

Except, the scar was populated. Lights on tall portable tripod units lit the entire area. In the center stood a derrick with platforms and equipment. Green storage tanks lined one side and gray storage tanks on the other. Lengths of pipe were laid out on racks. Red pumps of some sort surrounded the derrick, and big sand trucks as well as tractor trailer rigs were parked everywhere. It looked like an oilfield version of the ending scene in "Close Encounters of the Third Kind."

The noise of all the operating machinery was deafening. "What the hell is this?" I shouted to Salty, but he couldn't even hear me from the back seat.

We rounded the derrick and parked toward the back of the pad where worker housing trailers sat side by side. But beyond them, off the pad and in the low field, trailer after trailer lined the landscape. The noise level was a little lower back here, and I shouted to Salty, "What's with all the trailers?"

"Takes a lot of workers to drill a well and put a rig up."

I pointed out in the low field. "Not that many."

"Yeah, well, some are only with us for a little while."

Then it started to make sense. Simpson Drilling. Lon Claymore buying up land and drilling fracking wells, probably with as little safety oversight as the Pennsylvania ones. Plus, using the operation as a cover for illegals he was bringing in to use as workers. Or sell off to whomever could use them for whatever purpose suited them.

Salty pulled a sidearm out of his glove compartment, along with a holster, and strapped it on. He patted it for emphasis and said, "Come on, Pal. You and your friend are gonna start your tour now."

Bubba guffawed again. "Huh-huh. Start your tour now."

As I stepped down out of the cab, I saw that Salty left the keys in the ignition. Not that a breakaway seemed imminent or even possible. Still. A useful piece of information, I thought. I also noticed the white car with the Chihuahua plates. But next to it was another surprise. Baxter's Towne Car was parked beside it. My mind struggled to put more pieces of the puzzle together, but before I could ask another question, Salty grabbed my arm and pulled me forward, with Bubba doing the same to Akira.

"You got to be real careful around here, Pal. It's easy to get hurt," said Salty.

"Hurt easy." That was Bubba, of course.

"Accidents happen all the time."

"Accidents."

Bubba's verbal capacity seemed to top out at about three syllables.

"In fact, every so often, people disappear here and are never seen or heard from again."

"Never seen from again."

"Congrats, Bubba. That was six syllables." But Akira and I exchanged a worried glance. Things weren't looking too good. He still had his Aikido stick and I had my trained fists, but this was a fortress we had entered.

"Up we go." Salty and Bubba pulled us up an open metal stairway to a first level work area that looked out over the stacked pipes below and the entire terrain. Off to the back area, below the giant pad, I saw two huge lagoons. A pump spewed mud out of a drain hose into one of them.

"Hey, Salty. Aren't those pits supposed to be lined? You know, according to federal law and all?"

"The mud pits? There's some law about that, but there ain't nothing bad going in there. Just leftover bits and pieces and particles."

"As long as you're in the tour business, I think OSHA, the EPA and about a dozen other agencies might be interested in one of your getaway inspection packages."

"Yeah. Sure. Like they even know we're here." He pushed us into an enclosed area that had controls and measuring devices and lockers for the workers. "Bubba, you keep them here in the Dog House while I see if there's any accidents in the making." Then he stepped out.

Bubba stared at us and then started laughing. "You guys are in the Dog House."

"Good, Bubba. You made a joke. That's very good. Do you get it, Akira?" I nudged him with my elbow and we exchanged glances again, with the implication that this was it. Break now, or maybe not at all.

I made a slight move that caught Bubba's attention, and when he looked my way, Akira slowly raised his hand over his back to his Aikido stick. But just as he did, Salty reentered with sidearm in hand. Akira, just as slowly, lowered his hand, not willing to risk it.

"Guess what, Bubba? I think I just found the perfect accident waiting to happen."

"Perfect accident. Huh-huh." This guy had an endless capacity for insightful commentary. I wondered if he'd passed second grade.

Salty motioned with his sidearm for us to exit the Dog House and stand on the working area of the platform. There were metal gangways and catwalks heading off in all directions, but nowhere to run. At least nowhere to run for a safe getaway.

"Okay, Bubba. Start up the drill brake."

Bubba flipped a switch on a metal box with levers on it that controlled something, and gears and machine noise ratcheted up. This had me worried. Machinery in the hands of Bubba could only lead to catastrophic events of unparalleled proportions. A large round length of metal started rotating in a hole in the decking, extending above, through and below it.

"That there's a drill bit. Goes down through the Rat Hole, hundreds of feet into the ground." Salty holstered his sidearm, and walked over to a thirty foot length of drill pipe that rested against the platform's edge. He picked up the end of a long piece of heavy-duty chain and with one expert flick of the wrist, sent it wrapping several times around the pipe. When he pulled one of the levers, the chain sent the pipe sailing, violently, high into the air, to another platform that seemed suspended high above our heads.

"All the way to the Crow's Nest," said Salty. "Now, if that chain was to be wrapped around, say, somebody's leg, by way of an accident of course, ain't no way they'd survive. See what I mean about getting hurt easy around here?"

"Hurt easy." Bubba was starting to get on my nerves. My brain can only tolerate so many monosyllabic utterances without shutting down.

"Now you, Pal." Salty pointed to me. "You stand right over there where that pipe was leaning." He patted his sidearm. As I moved into position, he lowered the pipe, disengaged it, and let the chain drape on the deck next to me.

I looked at Akira. We both sensed that if we didn't make a move soon, despite the bleak outlook for success, we'd lose any chance at an escape. I was about to nod a signal for action when the drill bit that turned in the Rat Hole started rotating faster and faster. The ten inch tubing that pumped lubricating mud into the system began jumping in convulsions. Then the drill rod began shimmying back and forth. Next, I heard violent noises coming from below the platform. Over the side and below, I saw several men turn and look. Their expressions were not comforting.

"Oh, shit." Salty's eyes went wide. "Hydraulics. I forgot to turn on the blowout preventer." He bolted down the steps, but half way there, turned around and yelled at Bubba. "Turn off the drill. Hit the drill brake." Then he ran down and out of sight. Men now ran from several directions toward the base of the rig.

When I turned, there was panic in Bubba's eyes. He started for the drill brake, stopped and started again. But his foot hit the chain draped on the deck. He slipped, and the chain end flipped up and encircled his ankle. As he fell, his arm hit one of the levers and the chain instantaneously jerked up, pulling Bubba with it, him hanging upside down as he sailed high and violently all the way to the Crow's Nest. His inverted lifeless body flopped back and forth as the chain bounced high over us.

That's when the voices below us, under the decking, suddenly got louder. Much louder. Alarmingly louder.

"Valve seal. Valve seal," someone yelled.

Then another. "Valve seal washout."

Akira and I need no other bidding. We ran down the stairs, and as we did, the mud tubing broke loose, snaking around in the air and pumping streams of mud out onto the platform instead of into the system. Like a sudden drop in the barometer, I could feel the pressure plummet in the entire system, and then the platform itself started to shake with rumblings coming deep from within the earth. More screams of panic.

"Blow out. Blow out."

Men in hard hats ran out and away from the rig. Dark silhouettes, they darted about like moths preparing to hone in on an impending flame to self-immolate. We ran straight for the quad-cab where I knew keys awaited us in the ignition. I glimpsed the white car man emerge from an office trailer as we ran past his car, but noticed Baxter's Towne car was gone. We jumped in the quad-cab, spun out when I gunned it in reverse, and then sent up a rooster tail of dust as we sped across the well pad.

By the time we reached the end of the gravel access road and turned out on the two lane, the thunder of the explosion hit, vibrating both the truck and our internal organs. We stopped and looked back. Flames shot skyward in an orange and yellow and blue inferno. The night sky lit up with billowing fire and gasses and burning debris.

I could not begin to imagine the carnage that would litter this field when the final toll was taken.

33

Tiresias came to me in my dreams that night, with a bleak vision and a warning.

I had fallen into an exhaustive sleep after I returned from getting my truck, leaving the quad-cab on a deserted country road and taking Akira back to his hut. Now I lay in my own bed, in a lifeless sleep, spent and depleted of all energy as well as emotion.

The dream began just before dawn, and it took me to a netherworld of mixed cultures, mingling past and present, reality and myth. The myth was one my grandfather told me.

Nuada, king of the Tuatha de Danann, brings the stone of Fal to Ireland, and his sword is one of the four great treasures of the land. He is revered as the protector and defender of all. He sits on his throne with a white light around him, like a fleece of silver. But the Fir Bolg have challenged the Tuatha de Danann, and at the first battle of Mag Tuired, a Fir Bolg warrior named Sreng engages Nuada in combat and cuts off his hand.

Irish rule of sovereignty proclaims that physical imperfection disqualifies him from kingship. Because of his blemish, Nuada has a hand of silver fashioned, and thus regains his rule.

But strange intrusions shift my dream to a time warp and it no longer makes sense. It is no longer my grandfather's tale, but instead, a twisted clutter of unintelligible, jumbled images.

Nuada proudly examines his hand of power, finely wrought from silver. Suddenly, two Yakuza dressed in black sharkskin suits and wearing sunglasses, grab his arm and pin it to a flat tree stump. A third Yakuza, wearing sunglasses, but dressed in samurai clothing and armor, holds his katana sword over the silver hand. He raises the sword and prepares to sever the hand.

But Sondra, my wife, appears from the grave, smoking a cigarette and dressed in an evening gown. She stares at the samurai, who cannot complete the action until Sondra turns her back to him. Then, his sword comes down on King Nuada's wrist.

But when the silver hand falls to the ground, it turns into a severed claw of a turtle, and Nuada's body shapeshifts to a giant carapace, an inverted shell laying on its back, and Tiresias' head stretching out into a void.

My body bolted upright in bed. I was sweating and breathing heavily. I stumbled into the bathroom, put my head under cold running water and drank tap water from my cupped hand. I leaned on the counter, staring at myself in the mirror, slowly regaining my breath.

Daylight began to seep through the edges of the window shades, and when I returned to the bedroom, my foot touched something on the floor next to the bed. My jade turtle I keep on my nightstand lay on the hardwood floor. I must have knocked it off when I jumped out of bed. I picked it up. Its right rear claw was missing, broken off in the fall.

Then, my breathing started going wild again and a band started to tighten around my head. I picked up the small piece of severed claw. Both it and the leg had red smeared across them, like blood. I sat down on the edge of the bed, and that's when I noticed it.

Off to the side, on the floor, a knife like the one Fukumoto had his lackey use, had been stabbed into the floor. Its blade was covered in blood.

I ran to the living room and looked across at my open French doors. The lock had been broken. When I ran out into the garden, I could see Tiresias across the back yard near his sand pit. I ran to him, fearing the worst.

He lay on his belly, head out and feet extended. All of them. Intact. But his nose touched Lissie's shell. Her head and legs were all withdrawn, but blood smeared the right rear leg opening and her severed claw lay a few feet from her, a string tied around it.

*****

"Looks like a raccoon got the better of her."

I didn't offer an alternative suggestion to Dr. Selby, Chisholm's one and only in-town veterinarian, about the cause of Lissie's condition.

"Will she be okay?"

"Most critters recover from attacks like these. I'll let you know more later in the morning, but don't worry too much about it. I've seen a lot worse."

I stopped by Alex's office to let him know what had happened, and asked him to have a patrol car drive by a few times a day to check on my place. Then, I went by Janie's house. She was just leaving for school.

"Hi. What's up, Mr. O?" She talked to me through my rolled down window as my truck idled.

"I had an intruder at my place last night. It's probably better if you hold off on the chores for a few days until we know it's safe."

"Are you okay?"

"Sure, but..." I hesitated about telling her what happened to Lissie, but I figured she had a right to know."

"But what?"

"I'm okay, but Lissie was injured." I didn't go into the details, but I could see fear and hurt in Janie's eyes. "Doc Selby thinks she'll be fine. I'll give you an update on her condition after school today. Don't worry though."

As I drove off, I saw her standing on the curb in my rearview mirror. She had a faraway look. Maybe I shouldn't have told her.

Laura answered on her throwaway when I called using her cell phone. It seemed like such a convoluted way to communicate. I filled her in on the wellhead fire as well as my home invasion.

"Sounds like you've been a busy boy."

"How about you? Anything shaking at your end?"

"I've got a date tonight."

"That's not exactly what I meant."

"Oh, you mean that other little matter. The stockholder meeting info was a matter of public record. This is just hearsay. Supposedly, once Claymore took a hit from what the Yakuza released, he realized they were serious. They threatened him with more releases and he's going to meet their demands."

"Good. Maybe they'll get off my back now. So, is it one of your students?"

"What?"

"Your date. Is it one of your students?"

"You know I have a strict policy against that. They have to have been graduated for at least a year before I will even consider it."

"Ah, such rigorous standards you have, my dear."

After we hung up, I bought a morning paper and sat at the counter in Latte Dottie's sipping my cup of java. I'd scoured the paper, and the only mention of yesterday's conflagration was a five line sidebar story buried on the back page of the local news section. The cutline said "Wellhead Fire SW of Wichita." There was no mention of explosions or shooting flames or contamination or injuries or death. Nor did it mention Simpson Drilling, Lon Claymore or even the exact location of the fire. Only that it had been, as it put it, contained. The word contained bore no resemblance to what I had witnessed.

I wondered what it took to practice such deceit. Only someone like Lon Claymore had the clout to do it.

I sat pondering my next move, considering what had happened at my bungalow and that the Yakuza was seemingly after me again and that Lon and Baxter and their minions all had their agenda, too.

"Jimmy, you're lookin' a little weary. Rough night?"

"You don't know the half of it, Dottie."

Her steel gray eyes had as much compassion as she allowed herself, and her gravelly voice was a few notches lower on the sarcasm meter than usual.

"Well, you hang in there. Things is bound to get better. That's what I tell myself, anyways, even though I know otherwise. Bound to get better." She headed back through the swinging doors into the kitchen.

Bound to, I thought. Bound to. But I wondered. My bizarre dream and it's real life aftermath had left me disconcerted and as drained as when I'd collapsed on my bed last night.

One thing was certain, even though I didn't want to address it. I couldn't stand the guy, but the hour had come for more face-time with Lon.

34

Landscape workers were busy with fall cleanup when I drove, unnoticed, through Claymore's open gates. The day was cool, with a blue, cloudless sky. Charlene, dressed in Capris and a white sleeveless blouse, stood supervising, one hand on a hip, the other holding a half-empty rocks glass and swirling melting ice cubes in it.

She barked out imperial instructions to the workers, until she noticed me stepping out of my truck. Then her face pinched up and her eyes trained laser beams on me.

"We do not need you meddling around here, Mr. O'Reilly. Please turn around and drive out." She apparently considered that statement enough to get rid of me and looked back at her workers. It didn't.

I put on my silly Irish grin. "Why Miss Charlene, I just dropped in to say hello to my old friend, Lon. Thought we might relive a few-"

Her head snapped back around to me and her voice took on a hard edge. "Apparently, you are not an adept lip reader. Let me try again. Leave our property now, or I will call the police. You are not welcome here."

I kept smiling. So much so, my cheeks started hurting. "What a woman you are, Charlene. I swear, you are just like a faucet."

"A what?"

"A faucet. One minute you're running hot, the next minute you're running cold. You're a hard woman to read."

Lon, wearing khakis and a polo, came out the front door, his doughface jiggling. Charlene saw him and said, "I was just telling Mr. O'Reilly he needs to get off our-"

But Lon, without acknowledging her comment or looking at her, spoke right over her. "Jimmy, my good friend." He extended a hand for a hearty handshake. "I just mentioned to my wife last night, we ought to have you over sometime. Glad you dropped in." He ushered me up the steps, past a fuming Charlene, and in to the sunken living room. "What can I get you?"

"Nothing Lon. I just wanted-"

He held up a hand. "Pedro, bring Baxter in, please."

"I'd prefer it if we could talk alone."

"No, Jimmy. I'm glad you showed up. I was just preparing Baxter to go get you, so this works out well. I have a business proposition for you, and Baxter needs to be in on the discussion." Baxter appeared in his usual dark slacks, white long-sleeved shirt and tie, sans coat, and stood off to the side nodding his notice of appearance.

"Here it is, Jimmy. I need to hire you to ensure that certain items get to their correct destination, and also, to return some items you will receive in exchange. Very simple."

"I'm not a delivery boy."

"No, you are a licensed private investigator."

"I work as a skip tracer."

"But you are licensed by the State of Kansas."

"The answer is no."

"Let me clarify. Not only is there some risk involved in this venture, it is also a highly confidential mission. You are bound to client confidentiality, and I want none of my personnel involved should anything be made public. Other than Baxter here, who will deliver the items to you, that is the extent of our involvement. Then it is in your hands."

Suddenly, it dawned on me what he was doing. He wanted me to be the go-between for the payoff to the Yakuza, distancing himself from the entire affair.

"The answer is still no."

"I pay handsomely, and if my sources are correct, you stand to benefit from this yourself, if you understand my drift."

"My answer is still..." Then it hit me. I did understand his drift. With the payoff, the Yakuza would also be off my back. But then, that presupposed that he knew something about my predicament. I played my hand with an equally vague response.

"I can pretty well guess what I would be delivering, but I need to know what I would be bringing back and just how dangerous it is."

"There are certain documents that, if made public, could ruin not only my business, but also my political future. You don't need to know what they are and that's the way we will keep it."

"Let's suppose I agree to this business proposition."

"Now you're talking, Jimmy."

"I said, let's suppose. Let's also suppose that you have knowledge about certain happenings." I looked directly at Baxter. "For example, a certain fire that occurred yesterday."

Lon got a puzzled look on his face. Baxter remained stone-faced. I saw the morning paper on a side table, got it and read the five line side bar about the fire. Neither of their expressions changed. "Of course, what this fire article doesn't mention is dead and injured workers, contamination, or the exact location." Still, no change in facial expression. Could Baxter have left before the fireworks and know nothing? Could they both be clueless about it?

205

"Exact location," I said. "Like a wellhead in the Cimarron Breaks where a white car with Chihuahua plates and a black Lincoln Towne Car were parked next to each other, and scores of trailers were lined up to house transitory illegal immigrants."

Baxter's stone face crumbled, but Lon looked just as perplexed as before, and he said, "What the hell are you talking about?"

"Baxter knows what I'm talking about. Don't you, Baxter? You were there. Did you leave before it all erupted?"

"I think you picked the wrong man for the job, Mr. Claymore," Baxter said. "This guy's got a screw loose."

"I may have a screw loose, but I'm going to be a ten penny nail up your ass until the truth comes out. Your car was there yesterday, along with all the Simpson Drilling trucks and all their connections to Lon's company. You and I know it. Maybe you left before all hell broke loose, but you have a stake in all these doings. From illegals, to children being used for pornographic purposes, to women being sold into sexual slavery. What's your connection?"

I looked at Lon. "What does it take to cover something like this up? How much does it cost? Who do you have to know?" I felt a tension band starting to tighten around my head and my trapezius beginning to knot up.

Lon stood up. "What's all this about, Baxter?"

Baxter's eyes frantically searched for a way out. "I heard there was a small fire at one of our wellheads yesterday. Nothing serious though."

"I'm talking about the other things he mentioned. Women and children."

"I don't know shit about what he's talking about." Baxter was starting to lose his cool, and I was reveling in it.

"Your car was there. I saw it, and you know exactly what I'm talking about."

Lon looked at me and then at Baxter and back at me again. After a moment, he said, "Come with me, Baxter." And the two of them walked out of the room.

I stood up, trying to do some deep breathing exercises and regain both my composure and my concentration. A few minutes later, Lon walked back in with another one of his enforcers. I recognized him from the entourage at the Chisholm gym public relations charade.

"This is Randle. Randle is going to assist you in transferring the items we talked about."

"What happened to Baxter?"

35

What happened to Baxter remained to be seen. When I walked out of Lon Claymore's estate, a black Towne Car was exiting the gates and leaving ahead of me to parts unknown. At least to me.

Lon had given me the delivery boy instructions I'd acquiesced to, against my better judgment, but I still did not believe he was ignorant of all the sordid details I'd brought up. He had to have known something. Time would tell.

I stopped by Doc Selby's office to see how Lissie was doing, in hopes I could take her home and reunite her with Tiresias. Two Greek legends, together, again.

I was in for a surprise.

"She's doing just fine. She's going to have trouble getting around on three legs, but she'll be okay. We do need to keep her for observation for a couple of days, but that will give you some time. You might want to make your home compliant with the ADA, though."

"ADA?"

"American Disabilities Act." Selby winked at me. "If you don't have total turtle accessibility to parking, and upgrade your restrooms for handicapped turtle access with federally required modifications, they'll be breathing down your neck."

"Smile when you say that," I said.

He smiled. "There is one other little detail, Jimmy."

I pulled out my checkbook. "Okay, what's the damage, Doc?"

"Later, Jimmy. Later with that. I don't quite know how to put this, but, well, you're going to be a granddaddy."

"What?"

"Lissie's pregnant."

I stepped back and sat down. Stunned. "Pregnant? Lissie's pregnant? You sure?"

"Well, no animals were harmed in this test, but, you know. As they say, the rabbit died."

"Who's the father?" I said.

"You're going to have to ask Tiresias that question."

I drove home in a stupor. Two turtles in my back yard was a chore. A family would be... well, beyond me. I needed to research how many turtles come in a litter, or whatever they call turtle offspring. A flock of turtles. A pride of turtles. A gaggle of turtles. Turtles galore. Turtles out my ass.

When I got home, dusk was creeping in and I poured myself a glass of red and sat on my terrace thinking about turtle offspring, the Yakuza, Lon Claymore and my stupid cave-in to Lon's request to be his delivery boy. I pulled out Laura's cell phone and called her. No answer. Date time. Out prowling with the younger generation. Cougar at large. I dearly loved the woman, but had no idea what she was all about.

I dialed Janie's cell phone number. I didn't understand why a fourteen year old needed a cell phone. But then, I didn't understand how anyone did. I didn't even know why I was using Laura's cell phone instead of my landline inside.

"Janie. I just wanted to tell you, Lissie is going to pull through."

"Oh, that is such good news to hear. Thanks. I appreciate you letting me know, Mr. O. I've been so worried."

"One other thing. Doc Selby says she is going to have babies."

"Lissie's preggers? OMG. Oh, wow. That's fantastic. We'll have to have a celebration. A baby shower. You can host a baby turtle shower at your place."

"Yeah, well. We'll talk about that later." After we hung up, I sat on my terrace sipping my glass of red and contemplating my role in the universal scheme of things. Skip tracer. Delivery boy. Granddaddy to turtles. Potential host to a turtle shower. Maybe Akira could help me make sense of it all.

I looked down at Tiresias, who stared up at me, sightless, through the basil on my terrace.

"You old son-of-a-gun," I said. "I didn't know you had it in you."

I sat there trying to decide whether to fix myself something to eat or go in to town and have dinner at Dottie's. Before I could decide, the doorbell rang.

"Laura." I looked out beyond her and didn't see anyone else. "Where's your date?"

She stormed in past me and sat on the edge of the couch, fuming. She wore tight fitting jeans with silver studs around the front and back pockets and down the outside seams, along with a designer tee and an Ed Hardy belt adorned with skulls.

"The guy's a jerk."

I stared at skulls on the belt. "What was the occasion for the date? Grave robbing?" The humor didn't help.

"I thought we were going dancing and drinking. Turns out his idea of a good time is sitting on the couch playing video games all evening."

I sat down across from her. "Laura, maybe this generation gap thing is starting to take its toll. It's possible, just possible, you might want to alter your date criteria just a little. Say, to those within ten years of your age."

She leaned back in the couch and sighed. "I'm getting old."

"Old-er. And we all are. It's inevitable." I put some slow dance music on the CD player. "Care to dance?" We slow-danced a few numbers, her head on my shoulder.

"Okay. I'm better now." We sat back down. "Thanks. That helped."

I fixed some goat cheese crostini, with chopped black olives, tomatoes and basil, drizzled with some olive oil. We munched on those, and drank wine. I know she would have preferred a martini, but that's something I don't stock. After we commiserated about the downside of getting older, conversation wandered to the problems at hand.

"Lon Claymore has hired me to do a job," I said.

She stared at me for a few seconds. "Your childhood nemesis? And you said yes?"

"Well, it's a long story."

"Make it short. Who does he want found and what's he going to do to him when you find him, that you'll have that on your conscience?"

"It's not a skip trace job. You remember that little news update you gave me about the Yakuza demands and Claymore meeting them? Well, I'm the go-between. Buffer-boy, who delivers something and returns something so that Claymore can keep his hands clean and save his pretty political ass."

"And you get the added benefit of getting the Yakuza off your ass."

"Bingo."

"It's kind of like when you were in grade school. He's making you walk in and yell 'Eat Shit' to the world. You lose, either way."

"Yep."

"It stinks."

"Yeah, I know."

"I don't mean it just stinks. I mean, it really smells. Something's rotten here and we're nowhere near Denmark. You might not come out of this in one piece."

"After the fact, driving home, a similar thought occurred to me."

"Call him and back out."

"Not an option."

We sat, munched, sipped and discussed what options we did have and how to deal with them so that I might remain in one piece.

We had a plan, of sorts.

We should have had a plan B.

36

"The fun is just beginning, O'Reilly." This, the male voice of an "Unidentified Caller."

"Who is this?"

"You know who it is."

"How'd you get this number, Baxter?"

"The how doesn't matter. Let's just say I know people in high places. What matters is what happens next. You, me and Randle are going to have some fun." The phone went dead.

I looked around, clutching my North Face backpack with pink trim in one hand, as it dangled against my leg. It bulged with waded-up newspaper.

Somewhere, across a brightly colored sea of dancers, Randle was supposed to be waiting for me with his North Face backpack with pink trim. It bulged with wads of money. Apparently, Baxter was present, too. This complicated matters.

The very public exchange of our pink-trimmed backpacks was being effected at Nomar International Market at Twenty-first and Broadway, a point where diverse cultures meet and mingle in north Wichita. Southeast Asian markets, East Asian restaurants, Hispanic storefronts, Persian rug dealers and ethnic traders of all cultures could be found in the surrounding neighborhoods, but the predominant architecture and cuisine was Hispanic.

Today's festival was honoring the *Reina del Maiz*. The Corn Queen would be crowned after a parade, but right now, the wide concrete public square at Nomar contained a *Baile Folklórico* dance group. Men in black charro suits with vests and tight pants and silver buttons down each side, tapped and stomped the Mexican Hat Dance. While women dressed in multi-colored, ruffled and tiered skirts, and white China Poblano blouses, swirled their dresses at the mock dance courtship from the men.

Rhythms from a five piece Mariachi band drove the dancers on, as a violin, vihuela and guitar blended their sounds, a guitarron added bass notes, and a trumpet blared its brassy melody.

Smells of roasted peppers, warm tortillas, fresh cilantro and pico de gallo rose up from food vendors and carried on the breeze.

I still hadn't spotted Randle, or Baxter for that matter, and as I walked the perimeter scanning, I pulled Laura's cell phone back out to call her. She waited across the street where she had a better overall vantage point.

"I'm jealous. Who were you talking to, O'Reilly?" Laura answered my call.

"What's plan B, Laura?"

"We barely have a plan at all. What do you mean, plan B?"

"Baxter's in the house. He's got something planned, and we'd better have some alternatives."

"What's he up to?"

"I guess he's gone rogue. Jumped ship on Claymore and operating solo. He's got your, well my phone number, and he sounds like he's out for some kind of revenge on me."

"What have you ever done to him?"

"Other than knee him in the groin and insult him to his face multiple times both in private and public, not much." I could visualize her shaking her head.

"What can he do here? It's a public place. Find Randle, make the exchange and we'll go from there."

I had exactly forty-five minutes to make the exchange and get the money to Fukumoto. The clock was ticking and all I had was wadded up newspaper in a girly looking backpack.

Just then, I spotted Baxter. No wonder I hadn't noticed him before. He was out of uniform, wearing jeans and a tee. He stood, casually peeling corn husks back from a tamale, underneath the pavilion overhang of Nomar's hacienda style building. On the ground next to him was a pink trimmed backpack.

I started toward him and then stopped. If he already had the money, what was he waiting around for? Just to get me? Then, through the dancers, I saw Randle seated on a bench with his pink trimmed backpack next to him.

There we were, the three of us, each with our designer packs, set up like a triangle on opposing sides of the festivities. I wondered if Randle knew of Baxter's presence. I skirted the dancers and moved toward Randle, but suddenly Baxter disappeared.

My phone rang. "I can see all three of you from here," said Laura. "Keep circling around, heading toward Randle, but stay on the phone and I'll let you know what Baxter does."

"Where is he now?"

Before she could answer, Randle apparently sighted Baxter, because he stood, picked up his backpack, and moved. Then, I lost sight of him.

"Great," said Laura. "All three of you are rotating clockwise around the festivities."

"Kind of like a Timex ad. Take a licking and keep on ticking."

"Quit trying to be cute. Remember, our goal is to keep you in one piece."

"Oh, yeah. I'd almost forgot." I felt for my Ruger in my pocket holster, and patted it just for reassurance.

"Okay," said Laura. "They've both dropped off my radar. Do you see them?"

Somebody screamed. Loud enough to top the Mariachi music.

"I'm signing off." I ran, cutting through the tapping and swirling dancers to the far side of the party. A woman from a donation table for the Sisters of Perpetual Sorrows stood screaming next to a bench where others gathered. Randle slumped forward, with a shiv protruding from the base of his skull, and a backpack leaning against his leg.

I knelt down, unzipped the pink trim and stared at wadded up underwear. Now I had less than forty-five minutes, and two backpacks filled with wadded-up paper and scrunched-up underwear. Our me-in-one-piece-goal seemed more and more remote.

I saw a police patrolman running toward the screaming woman, so I picked up my pack and started circling the dancers, looking for Baxter. He was back under the pavilion overhang, casually leaning against a support post, presumably waiting for me. The moneyed backpack sat on the cement next to him.

The building gave me the luxury of cover to do an end-around and come up behind Baxter. I hit his redial on the phone and waited around the corner of the building for him to answer.

"It took you long enough." Baxter

"You think you pulled a fast one, don't you?" Me.

"Only half of a fast one. The other half is waiting for you. I got another little pointy object and it's got your name on it. All we got to do is locate your skull."

"Don't get too excited, and don't move. Right now a sniper's got you in his sights. You don't think I came here alone, do you? Look up over the dancers at that skinny building by the railroad tracks. Second floor, third window in."

He bit. As his gaze moved to the building and searched for the window, and as he squinted with concentration, I moved in behind him, switched the pink trimmed backpacks, moved back behind the building and waited.

"There's nothing there."

"Dang. I could have sworn I saw a sniper up there. Speaking of nothing there, you might want to check your backpack."

I hung up and ran like hell.

37

Stupid, stupid, stupid.

Why did I have to taunt him with the check-your-backpack comment? It's like I never learn. And now I was caught in the crowd and he was somewhere behind me. I kept looking over my shoulder.

I heard sirens in the distance, but they were going to have a devil of a time getting here. In fact, I was having a devil of a time getting to Laura with the backpack full of money.

I could see her across the street standing on a bus stop bench, and she could see me over the tops of heads. But in-between, the street was now lined on both sides with cheering spectators, several people deep. The parade had begun and clogged the street as its cars were bumper to bumper, with the Corn Queen and her attendants all smiling and waving, each from her respective vintage convertible, perched high on the top of the backseat.

I nudged in to the edge of the crowd and then pushed harder. It was not only useless, but in addition, onlookers were starting to swarm in behind me. I was trapped. If Baxter and his little pointy object found me, I'd be shivved from behind, drop to the ground and no one would even notice or give a shiv, so to speak, until he was long gone with the money.

"*Señor* O'Reilly." My name rang out loud and clear over the crowd noise. "*Señor* O'Reilly."

I spun around and Inez Gonzalez waved at me and kept calling my name. I tried to signal her to stop, but she didn't get it and it was too late anyway. Baxter had heard and pushed his way toward me. I felt for the Ruger, but I couldn't use it in a crowd like this.

As Baxter weaved and pushed through the crowd, I called Laura and gave her a heads-up. A sort of mini-plan B.

Baxter stopped short and smiled a wicked smile.

"Gee, I didn't know you could smile, Baxter."

He kept up the smile and mimed sticking a shiv in the air, like it was up my skull, and then he eyed the money pack.

I held up my hand and said, "I got another sniper."

"I fell for it the first time, scumbag. What's the saying? Once shot, twice shy?"

I didn't correct him, although I wanted to grab my crotch and say, "Bite me." Instead, I pointed behind me toward Laura, and said, "See her?"

Laura, still on top of the bus stop bench, raised her arms like she was waving a cheer for the Corn Queen. In doing so, her shirt clung to her body, outlining her under-the-shirt shoulder holstered Glock. Then, with one hand, she mimed taking out the gun, pointing her finger-barrel at Baxter, popping a round off and then blowing imaginary smoke off her finger tip. She smiled at him.

"See?" I said. "A sniper. She can smile, too."

Baxter started laughing and took a step toward me.

"Her underwear has crossed rifles embossed on them," I said.

Evidently he understood the significance of panties with the Marksman symbol imprinted on them, because he stopped short again and his smile faded. "She wouldn't," he said. "Not in a crowd like this."

"She would. She has. Her Marksmanship award is for rifles. But she's just as deadly with a handgun. And quick. In case you're interested, it's a Glock 19."

He scanned the crowd and slowly backed off a couple of steps. I could see him thinking though options, and then looking for Inez Gonzalez as a possible hostage to counter the turn of events, but luckily, Inez had been swept along in the current of onlookers, downstream from us. He faded back into the crowd and pulled the shiv out, brandishing it at me as a last taunt.

I only hoped that he had not been privy to where the final transaction with Fukumoto was going to take place.

38

I stood looking down the dusty Main Street of Old Cow Town.

This was Fukumoto's choice of venue for the transaction. Laura and I had paid our admission and entered separately, and she disappeared, observing the happenings from some unknown location. I hoped she'd be ready when all hell broke loose, as I was sure would eventually happen.

Old Cow Town is a tourist attraction. It is a re-creation of a late eighteen hundreds frontier town with a dirt main street that cattle would have been herded down at the end of a drive. It sits back a ways from the confluence of the Big and Little Arkansas Rivers where the Keeper of the Plains stands, and it is closer to the Big's side. On any given day, hordes of locals, as well as out-of-towners, congregate on the boardwalk near storefronts to watch any of several reenactments, including a cattle drive, shootouts, bank robberies, and trade displays such as blacksmithing and roping. Little tykes get officially deputized and are given a real tin star. The place was packed that afternoon.

I stood at one end of Main Street, outside the parsonage next to the First Presbyterian Church, my pink trimmed backpack full of greenbacks slung over one shoulder. I scanned Main Street, down one side past the harness and saddle shop, the marshal's office and the bank. Then I looked up the opposite side past the drugstore, barber, newspaper and funeral parlor. Kids played shootout with imaginary guns, weaving in and out of teenagers on dates and entire families out for the afternoon fun.

Then suddenly, Fukumoto stepped out from behind a boardwalk post at the far end of the street, near the drugstore. He sauntered into the middle of the street, turned and squared off facing me at the other end. He wore a black ten gallon hat and a white long sleeved shirt with a black satin vest, black chinos and black and tan hand tooled cowboy boots. A six-gun was strapped around his waist, appearing like the fake guns everyone else sported, but I knew better. He looked like an Asian Black Bart ready for a fast draw showdown.

This guy lived in a fantasy world that no reality TV show could even begin to capture. To compound it, School Girl suddenly appeared out of nowhere and stood at his side. She still wore her silly school girl outfit, but now sported a red cowgirl hat, tilted back over her black bangs and pigtails. She dragged a pink trimmed backpack behind her, presumably with the documents I was supposed to receive for Lon, in exchange for the money. If I'd invested in pink trimmed backpacks, I'd be millionaire by now.

I set my backpack down on the ground next to me, and Fukumoto eyed it with a deadpan, poker-faced stare. School Girl slouched next to him.

When did these guys lose touch with reality and what planet did they come from? I waited for Fukumoto to draw on me, not knowing what to expect out of this Theatre of the Absurd moment, when all of a sudden, the stakes shifted.

Rice pelted the back of my head.

"Good luck."

"Have a great life."

"Good-bye. Good-bye and good luck."

Yells and screams of good cheer filled the air as a wedding ceremony, a real-life one, not a reenactment, concluded in the First Presbyterian Church next to me. The bride and groom ran out into the sunny street, she in her white gown and he in his black tux, and began their post-ceremony promenade down the middle of Main Street for their honeymoon departure. Fukumoto balked, but he held his ground.

It looked like the opening scene from "High Noon," except the bride looked nothing like Grace Kelly and I couldn't do a Gary Cooper imitation to save my life.

With more and more revelers from the wedding party following the newlyweds, tossing rice and yelling good wishes, the street was getting clogged with people. Fukumoto wanted a public exchange, but I could see this was getting a little too public for him. His eyes darted back and forth and I saw a little panic creep into them as he realized he was no longer in control. Suddenly, he nodded to me with his head to follow him, and he and School Girl moseyed past the drugstore and down a side street.

I moseyed right along after them, following them into a newly constructed building, soon to be a replica school house. It was one room, and the smell of freshly cut lumber and sawdust filled the air. Sawdust lay on the plank floor, and the only objects in the room were two sawhorses, a rickety chair and a few boards. Two windows had been framed, but boarded up, so the place was dark and cool inside.

"Howdy, Pardner." This was Fukumoto. I had never contemplated what "Howdy, Pardner" said with Japanese accent would sound like. It wasn't pretty.

"Do you honestly believe you're living in the Old West?" I said.

"Yep. Git your caboose on over here, O'Reilly. Let us conclude our business here and be on our way before sundown."

This guy was unbelievable. "Quickly," I said, although I didn't move. The quicker I could distance myself from these sleazebags, the better.

"Oh, how you Americans are always in such a hurry. We, on the other hand, prefer to talk around the issue. Speak only through implication and let the outcome arrive indirectly."

"Well, here's the money." I pushed the backpack into the middle of the room. "How's that for indirectness?" I moved off to one side and kept my distance.

Fukumoto frowned, clearly upset that he was not going to get to play out his Old West fantasy. He nodded to School Girl and she went to the middle of the room, unzipped the backpack, verified its contents, and nodded back to him. Then she stood, left her backpack sitting next to mine and returned to his side.

"Does she ever talk?" I said.

"Occasionally, when she has something important to say, and I allow her to."

We all stood, staring at the backpacks. Fukumoto spoke first.

"I suppose you would like to examine the contents of your package. However, it really doesn't much matter. You see, Mr. O'Reilly, I have no intention of allowing you to leave here alive. All that remains is the matter of your disposal."

I had been anticipating something along these lines and had my hand in my pocket on my Ruger, but he preempted me. "Don't even consider that," he said, staring at my pocket and tilting his holstered six-shooter to aim it directly at me. "Otherwise, your allotted time will be even shorter." I withdrew my hand, my mind racing over what my next move might be.

Then, out of nowhere, came an unfamiliar voice.

"Don't move, or I shoot everybody."

All three of our heads snapped toward the door. There stood Toshi's counterpart from the cinderblock porn shop raid. The fully clothed one with tattoos sprouting out the shirt. He had a nine in each hand, one pointed at me and the other at Fukumoto.

"Yuji?" Said Fukumoto. "What are you doing? This is not like you. Give me those weapons." He took a step toward Yuji, but Yuji raised the nine at Fukumoto's head.

"Hand over the backpack if you want to stay alive."

"Which one?" said Fukumoto, and he nodded at the side-by-side twin packs in the middle of the floor.

Yuji looked at both of them, and seemed to get confused. He clearly hadn't been prepared for this. Fukumoto took the opportunity to draw his six-shooter and level it at him. Yuji stepped back with panic in his face, all his traitorous plans unraveling. But just as these swift twists of events took place, yet another strange reversal of fortune occurred.

School Girl executed a quick and stunning martial arts move. She spun, did a high leg kick that knocked Fukumoto's gun from his hand and into the far corner of the room, and then joined the newcomer, Yuji, standing by his side.

"I think she just said something important," I said to Fukumoto.

"I glad you come, Yuji." This was School Girl. "I afraid you not keep promise."

"Now she's really, truly, actually talking," I said.

"I always keep my promises, Shizuko. Especially when money is involved." Yuji put one arm around School Girl, who now had a name. Shizuko. "And also, especially for you, my sweetie."

Ah. True love. How sweet it is, I thought.

Fukomoto, to his credit, kept his composure. "What are you doing, Shizuko? How dare you be disloyal? Come back over here immediately."

"No." She defiantly straightened her red cowgirl hat that had gone askew from the kick.

"I command you."

"I say no. How you think I like being nothing but your arm candy?"

"Being what?"

"What American call arm candy. I hear them call me that. That all you think I am. Not so. I more than arm candy. I have mind."

Whew. She not only spoke. She unloaded.

Fukumoto tried some leverage. He spoke directly to Yuji. "This is something you do not want to do. You know I am boss, but I am only a *wakagashira*. If you kill me, they will only send another *wakagashira*, or worse for you, a *saiko komon*, senior advisor. You will be hunted down and killed. There is no escape, and you know it."

"We'll take our chances." Yuji.

"Yes. We take chances." Shizuko.

Then, just as swiftly as her other move, Shizuko whipped the belt off of her pleated school dress and had it around Fukumoto's neck. She wrangled him into the lone chair, forced him down and into it and began tightening the belt, choking him.

He screamed, but outside, clanging from a blacksmith demonstration and kids yelling, drowned out his noise.

I saw movement in my peripheral vision and turned to look in the corner. There, a wolf spider came out from under a board on the floor, backwards, turning in circles as it pulled its hairy eight-legged, mottled brown body out. Then, a larger mate, a male, followed. The male preened, as he danced and pranced his showy self off to his partner. He went into a courtship dance, waving his front legs and vibrating his abdomen.

I read somewhere that wolf spiders don't have webs. They don't lay in wait for their meals. They are predators, seeking out their victims and then ambushing them.

I looked back at the threesome. Fukumoto gasped for air, but Shizuko pulled and twisted the belt tighter until a gurgling sound came out of his mouth. His feet pounded the floor as he fought for physical leverage, but Yuji grabbed both ankles and held them down.

Fukumoto's arms flailed and the chair bounced, but she kept the pressure up until he finally went limp.

I looked back in the corner. The male wolf spider had gone into a paroxysm of showy dance. The female became so excited, she advanced on him, attacked and carried him off under the board. I looked at Fukumoto's limp body and wondered what fate awaited the male spider.

The two human lovers had all but forgotten me as they finished up with Fukumoto. I knew they would turn their attention to me next, and I had no thoughts of waiting around to find out what they had in mind. With their attention on Fukumoto's body, I slowly made my way to the backpacks, wrapped one hand around each and silently finessed my way back out the door. I knew they wouldn't be far behind.

In fact, as I headed back toward Main Street, I recalled yet another detail about wolf spiders. They could occasionally be seen walking across the surface of water, in hot pursuit of prey that had eluded them and fallen in.

For the second time that day, I ran like hell.

39

Laura didn't answer her cell phone. Not good.

As I ran, awkwardly balancing one backpack on each shoulder, I dialed Charlie's number next, at WPD. "Homicide. Detective Daniels." Thank God she was at her desk.

"It's me, Charlie." I huffed as I ran, out of breath. "There's a 10-40 at Cow Town in the new school house they're building."

"Bruiser? You? Involved in a fatality report? Why am I not surprised? What have you done now, O'Reilly?"

"You ask too many questions. Just get down here now. This is ongoing. Ain't over yet, Charlie." I ended the call just as I came up on Main Street.

I stopped, scanned the area, and didn't see anyone but the crowds of locals and tourists. I looked back over my shoulder. No Shizuko and Yuji. Yet. I knew it wouldn't be long, though. It might be true love, but somehow I suspected that money is what fueled Yuji's passion. The old Groucho Marx saying popped into my mind. "Love flies out the door, when money comes innuendo."

I walked down the boardwalk looking for any sign of Laura, hoisting my backpacks and huffing to catch my breath. Nothing. And there wasn't time to go searching the entire Cow Town park.

Just then, a bank robbery reenactment began its performance for the delight of the crowd. It was one of the favorites of both the locals and the tourists, and they all stopped to watch the staged event.

One member of the gang held the horses in the middle of Main Street, while directly opposite the drug store, three desperados backed out of the bank door, fake money sacks in hand and fake guns drawn. A pretend teller came running out after them trying to steady a replica Colt between his two shaking hands and firing the blanks in it.

"You won't get away with this, you miserable, low-down-"

The robbers' guns blazed away, with the teller falling, wounded, on the boardwalk, but he returned fire as he went down and one of the robbers fell, too.

Kids jumped up and down, screaming and yelling at all the drama of this theatrical event. Parents watched in amazement, with fathers proudly pointing out historically accurate details they could identify.

Baxter intentionally chose this moment to make his entrance, emerging from the harness and saddlery shop. So, he was privy to where the final transaction was taking place. And with him, surprise, surprise, was none other than the white car man.

"What made you do it? What made you go rogue?" I yelled to Baxter. "Money? Greed? You'll never get away with this." Suddenly I realized I sounded just like the actors up the street, and I added, "You miserable low-down-"

But he was having none of it. The two of them had Laura pinned between themselves. How they had managed to physically restrain her, I'll never know, but Baxter held one of her arms tightly, twisting and manipulating her, as he offered her presence up to me as bait. It looked as if he might have had a gun in her back as well.

If Yuji and Shizuko showed up now, well, the complications were too intricate to fathom. All I had to leverage was the innocent bystanders, and I doubted any of the others involved cared about them at all. And no, I wouldn't risk kids' lives for mine or Laura's or Lon's money and incriminating documents.

Suddenly, I realized I did have an advantage. I held up both pink trimmed backpacks, one on each side of me, above my head.

Baxter and the white car man looked at them. Then, they scanned the street, not sure what to do.

"How'd you like the goods?" I dangled the backpacks in the air, taunting him. "Guess which one it is." He shoved Laura forward and off the boardwalk, into the street, as an offering to trade, and yes, he did have a pistol in hand. No one even noticed, or else they thought it was just part of the ongoing festivities. We strode toward each other with our prized possessions to trade, like two kids with their marble bags.

But when we were about forty paces apart, Yuji and Shizuko rounded the corner of the drugstore onto Main Street, eyed us and came to a dead halt. Then they started advancing toward us. With Baxter and sidekick on one side of me and the lovers on the other, both closing in, I did the only thing I could do.

I tossed each backpack into the middle of the street, about halfway between each twosome.

Now, everyone froze. No one knew what to do, and no one knew which bag had the money, including me. I'd lost track.

All this, along with the fake gunfight in progress, and Yuji panicked. He began yelling and running toward the backpacks while firing his gun off into the air, and with Shizuko following. Baxter and friend moved in, too.

That's when Laura and I made our move. I nodded to her. "We'll each take two," I said.

"Which two do you want?" she said.

"You take the lovers."

"Okay. Which two are the lovers?"

I rolled my eyes and headed for Baxter. He was an easy take-out. One punch to the solar plexus, he went down and his gun flopped out of his hand.

"You missed a few of your gym workouts, Baxter. You'd better get back with the program." The white car man was another story. He must have had training, because he proved as formidable as Flannel-man.

While we traded blows, I could see Laura dealing with Yuji and Shizuko. She'd kicked his one nine out of his hand, but he still had a holstered one. She was having her problems, as they countered her every move.

"Damn," she yelled over to me. "School Girl's a little whirling ninja."

"School girl's got a name," I said. "It's Shizuko."

"It's always good to know your enemy."

"Let me introduce you to her boyfriend. Yuji."

I was still grappling with the white car man, but I could tell it took all Laura's Aikido expertise just to counter the *ki* of each of them, much less advance or gain the advantage.

The gunfight was winding down with the robbers heading out of town, and I could tell the onlookers were starting to wonder about the strange fight that still raged on the streets of Cow Town.

That's when things got stranger.

At the far end of Main Street, who should suddenly appear, but Akira. I could see him over Baxter, as Baxter struggled to get his breath and rise to one knee. Akira. He'd appeared once again, out of nowhere.

Akira, dressed in his white, flared-out Yamabushi *suzukake* clothing, stood in an exaggerated pose, with one leg thrust back and the other forward and bent. One hand rested on his rear hip, elbow out, with the other hand holding his Aikido stick high in the air and pointed toward us, his head in alignment.

It looked like the set of a combined movie shoot for "The Magnificent Seven" meets "Seven Samurai."

Akira grasped the stick with both hands, and began a low rolling growl that built to a bizarre scream as he charged toward us, feet pounding on the dirt.

Yuji, still in panic mode, fumbled for his holstered nine, which left Laura free to deal with Shizuko alone. But Yuji dropped the gun and Akira was on him before he could recover. Akira and his *jo* took care of Yuji in short order.

While I struggled, throwing and countering punches, Baxter regained his breath and his footing, picked up both backpacks and started to attempt a quick exit, thinking he could just sneak off. But Akira, finished with Yuji, turned on him and charged. Just as he did, the stagecoach demonstration began its hourly run through town and came barreling around the corner onto Main Street. By the time the driver saw us, it was too late to reign in the horses, so he altered course to one side, trying to race past us.

"Stop now." Akira yelled, as he charged Baxter.

But Baxter was oblivious to everything except the money and getting way. One of the lead horses clipped him, knocking him down, and as he fell, the front wheel of the stagecoach ran over his left leg. We heard the crunch of bone being pulverized as Baxter screamed and lay in the dust in agony.

By now, we could hear the sirens approaching from my call to Charlie. The white car man heard them too, recognized the futility of fighting and took off running toward the entrance, playing right into the hands of WPD.

"Game's over, Shizuko," I said. I'd finally found a use for my Ruger, pulled it from its pocket holster and leveled it at her.

She apparently thought she was a character from "Crouching Tiger, Hidden Dragon," and could fly around bullets, because she started to execute a maneuver to charge me and my Ruger.

But Laura reacted instantly and made a quick take-down.

Laura, Akira and I all looked at each other in silence. The spectators all stood, mouths open, in silence. The stagecoach had stopped at the far end, and its driver looked back, in silence.

All quiet, on the western front.

The next sound anyone heard was Charlie's voice.

"What the hell have you done now, O'Reilly?"

40

"Damn, this shit is good."

This was Alex's reaction to his first taste of Boulevard Pale Ale.

"Don't you like having a friend who introduces you to finely crafted beer?" I said. "So you don't have to drink that turtle piss from a can."

"I'd like it better if that friend was on my staff. The position is still open. The offer still stands. You be one a my officers, you'd be pullin' in a salary."

"The answer's still the same. It's something I just can't do. Sorry, Alex."

"I understand your reasons, but it's not like our little berg's the violence capitol of the world. We mostly just deal with public intoxication and traffic violations."

"And the occasional body found in a field," I added.

"Yeah, well, that too." He drained the second half of his bottle and we got another round from the bottles iced down in my kitchen sink.

Earlier that day, the two of us had driven out to the field by Wiley's place and stood, looking at where the twenty-seven bodies had lain on cots in their body bags, just a few weeks before. The Indian Grass and Big Bluestem waved in the breeze, peacefully, as if no death had ever taken place there at all.

Neither of us said anything. We just looked, and I thought of how the land abides. No matter the human tragedies that come and go, the land still abides. As we watched, cattle egrets landed and began scavenging the field.

Now, back at my place, we guzzled pale ale and talked about how it all ended.

"Them bodies, every one of 'em, was claimed by someone back in Mexico," said Alex. "Every soul has found a resting place. Something I wouldn't have ever figger'd on."

"Inez Gonzalez came to see me yesterday," I said. "She is going through legal channels to try and get Maria, Little Julio and Elena here legally. She knows it's an uphill battle and will take a long time, but she's confident she'll succeed. Laura's helping her," I added.

"It is amazing what people will do to come to this country. To try and make a better life for themselves."

I nodded in agreement.

"Them two young Asians, what's their names?"

"Shizuko and Yuji," I said.

"Yeah. I never could pronounce names like that. Anyways, they're sittin' in the county jail. It don't look too good for them."

"No. But they'll get what they deserve. They killed a man, you know."

"A man that deserved it," he said. "That Fukimotor, or whatever his name is, was one mean SOB. I just don't get this Baxter guy, though. What the hell was he thinking?"

The last either of us saw of Baxter, he sat in a courtroom in a wheelchair awaiting arraignment. His left leg stuck straight out in a full cast from foot to hip, and a neck brace jacketed his head so he could only look straight forward.

"He figured he could cut his ties with Lon Claymore and walk away with a tidy sum and live happily ever after," I said.

"Like I said, it is amazing what people will do."

Although Salty still remained at large, in all likelihood, Baxter and the white car man, now known as one Dennis Langston who had been wanted for several years on a human trafficking warrant, would spend a long time behind bars for their misdeeds. The arraignment listed charges from human trafficking to aiding and abetting prostitution and child pornography. Not to mention their yet to be determined role in multiple deaths, be they homicide or manslaughter.

In fact, the extent of Lon Claymore's involvement and his ultimate fate were also undetermined. I couldn't stand the guy, yet his life was pitiable. Disgusting, but pitiable.

*****

A week later I held what I refer to as a "Case Closed" celebration at my bungalow. Laura and Akira attended, of course. I also invited Janie and her mother, Francine. Since Francine couldn't come, Janie asked if she could bring Zoey, along with W.B.

When they arrived, W.B. bounded through the front door, and immediately out the French doors looking for Tiresias on the terrace. Zoey's mother dropped them off. She walked in with a swagger, dressed in a white sundress and sandals, her brunette hair flowing down over her shoulders and a twinkle in her eyes.

Then, a miracle occurred. Zoey actually spoke. Cheerfully. And more than one word, even.

"Hello, Mr. O'Reilly."

"Hello, Zoey. How are you?"

"Kinda bummed. I think it's from the sun spot explosions."

"Oh, sure," I said. I had no idea what she meant.

"Don't you think it's ironic?" she said.

"The sun spots?"

"No. You know," she explained. "About Lissie being pregnant. She sure didn't live up to her name. I mean, obviously, she sure didn't go on any sex strike." She held up two rolls of crepe paper, one blue and one pink. "Janie and I thought we'd help celebrate."

Ah, teenagers. You just never know.

"This is Zoey's mom," said Janie, by way of a teenage introduction.

"Does Zoey's mom have a name?" I said.

"Candice. I'm Candice Morrison." Zoey's mom stepped forward, stuck out her hand and gave me one heck of a firm handshake.

"Do you go by Candy?"

"Nope. Just plain Candice."

"Candice it is, then." Although she didn't seem too plain to me. "I'm Jimmy O'Reilly," I said. "Won't you stay and join us? We have more than we can eat, and your company would be appreciated." I noticed how her sundress flared out at the thighs, and I think she caught me staring.

"Thank you, James. That would be nice."

James? No one had called me James since I was seven years old. Then, she flashed a big smile at me. At least, I think she did.

Janie and Zoey strung up the blue and pink crepe paper streamers so the party doubled as a turtle baby shower.

We all sat on the terrace and ate burgers I grilled, made from local grass fed beef. We watched as W.B. trounced around the back yard, nosing Tiresias and Lissie, taunting them and trying to goad them into a chase. But my two turtles weren't interested. They now had a life of their own, and a family on the way.

In fact, Lissie had been returned by Doc Selby with a prosthetic leg. He'd fitted her with a furniture wheel dolly that he screwed into the bottom of her shell. As long as I kept the grass short, she had no trouble maneuvering around the backyard at all.

Candice and I sat on the terrace observing the festivities, with the two teenagers teasing W.B.

"Janie and Zoey seem to be such good friends," I said.

"I think Janie's been a good influence on her," said Candice. "Zoey's had a few problems at school recently."

"I guess it is probably difficult, being a widow and raising a teenage daughter by yourself."

"Oh, I'm not a widow. My husband left us five years ago right after we moved to Chisholm. Ran off with the school secretary."

Dumb, I thought. That was a really dumb move O'Reilly. I vaguely recalled the gossip I'd heard at Dottie's about it at the time. Quite the town scandal.

"But it's not so tough," she added. "Zoey's a good kid. Just a little rebellious. Like me."

"So, that's where she gets it from. How about her love of poetry?"

"Me again," she said. "In fact, you and your terrace and herbs and garden remind me of a poem I love. It's so peaceful here." Then she quoted from Under Ben Bulben. "Know when all words are said / And man is fighting mad / For an instant he stands at ease / laughs aloud, his heart at peace."

"Yeats," I said. But I was wondering how she could know that about me. The fighting mad and heart at peace part.

"Well, I cheated. Janie told me he's one of your favorites."

I didn't say it, but I thought about the ending lines from the stanza. "Before he can accomplish fate / Know his work or choose his mate." Yikes. This was getting scary.

Akira and Laura interrupted us, bringing out dishes of vanilla ice cream topped with hot fudge and hazelnuts.

Later, as we cleaned up, Janie caught me and winked one of her squinty winks. "Looks like you and Mrs. Morrison have really hit it off. Nice going, Mr. O." She nudged me with her elbow.

I blushed.

41

Lon Claymore lost the election.

He was never indicted for anything. He never even was accused of anything. Apparently he knew nothing of Baxter's scheme bringing in illegal aliens and using them for labor in Claymore's businesses, as well as dealing off children for porn and women for prostitution for his own gain and profit. And he managed to obscure the bribery claims in the Pennsylvania case so that no one was ever charged.

If it hadn't have been for the fact that Robert Townsend, the trucker whose body we discovered with the missing finger, had found out the sordid details of how the women and children in his cargo were going to be used, none of this ever would have come to light. He threatened to go to the authorities, so Dennis Langston and the Yakuza took care of him, and then when they parceled out the cargo, Langston promptly botched his end of the job with the twenty-seven men.

But the events that actually did in Lon Claymore's political ambitions were the revelations of his total disregard for, and the non-compliance with safety standards, as well as the pollution and environmental havoc he had wreaked on workers and land alike. When OSHA and the EPA were made aware of the wellhead fire and its deaths and devastation, as well as other Claymore Oil disasters, they both went after him with a vengeance, and his beloved public turned on him so hard and so fast, you could watch the false charisma drain out of him like dirty suds down a sink.

I have no idea what was in the sealed envelope I'd gotten from Fukumoto, but its contents never came to see the light of day. If they had, I'm sure Claymore's fate would have been much worse.

I visited him one morning after the election. His gate stood open. There were no workers scrambling about his massive lawn or pool. He and Charlene sat on their porch, he staring off in the distance, and she nursing a bourbon on the rocks.

He stood and shook my hand and smiled, but it was an empty smile and his voice was flat. And those eyes. The eyes of Lon Claymore. They still held the vacant, amoral look they'd always had, only now with a look of defeat in them.

"Welcome, Jimmy. So good to see you. I've been meaning to send you that check for your services. Sorry about that." Charlene remained both seated and silent, not looking at me.

"That's not why I came," I said. "I-" In fact, I wasn't really sure why I had come. I would have liked to have told him off for a childhood incident that remained with me to this day. I would have liked to have told him what I thought of his kind and how they ruined so much of what was good in the world with their disregard and callous, self-serving deeds. But I didn't.

A realization came over me as I stood there. The fear I felt as a fourth grader when he and his cohorts commanded me to walk into the library and shout an obscenity, was no longer with me. Lon Claymore no longer held power over me, internally or externally. I was not the "bullied kid" anymore.

"A long time ago, you once asked me to say something. I couldn't do it at the time," I said. "But I think I can now."

"Really? What's that?"

"Eat shit."

He looked at me strangely, and Charlene's eyes got big as she finally looked my way.

We parted. I left behind a sad, defeated man. Yet one that most likely would rise up, rebuild his empire and continue to find ways to control those around him and run the world as he always had. His kind always did.

Later that week I went to the Cimarron Breaks and stayed with Akira for a few days. He completed the period of mourning for his son, and scattered ashes in the hills.

We talked of our departed wives. We sat on his plateau and watched red skies at sunset, that held cumulous clouds with purple bruises. Early mornings brought orange, cloudless skies and I felt limitless in their expanse. The likes of Lon Claymore faded from my consciousness there.

One evening, at sunset, I thought I saw the buffalo that Akira had seen in his vision, except that they were not dead, but alive and roaming the prairie. In their midst, a white buffalo calf stood by himself. Native Americans considered a rare birth of a white bison to be sacred, and to be a symbol of hope and unity.

"Would you do what you did that one time?" I said to Akira. "When you laid your hands on me and I felt so peaceful."

"No," was all he said. Instead, he stood and preformed some sort of ritual, and I saw exploding colors and felt myself float away in a ball of bright yellow energy.

"What was that all about?"

"I did a *Reiju*. What you call a Reiki attunement in the West. Now, place your hands on your heart."

I did.

"Now, give yourself Reiki."

"I can't."

"You just did."

And as I sat there, hands on my heart, I felt an explosion of energy, and a calm, peaceful feeling came over me.

Somewhere, out in the darkening hills of the Cimarron Breaks, a coyote yammered. But it wasn't a complaint.

It was an acceptance.

*****

About the author: Conrad Jestmore has published short stories, poetry and non-fiction in numerous journals and anthologies, and is a Past President of Kansas Writers Association. His first Jimmy O'Reilly murder mystery, *River of Murder*, is available as an e-book and in paperback from his website, www.conradjestmore.com. His poetry chapbook, *Roadmap to Hope*, is available directly from the author. He has earned gainful employment as a welfare case worker in the mountains of northern California, an elevator operator when elevators still had them, a bartender, a paint warehouse stocker, a USO performer and a high school teacher. He is a Reiki Master and currently teaches Reiki classes and heals both humans and animals in his central Kansas Reiki practice.